D0016457

A Mother's Love

A MOTHER'S LOVE

Mary Morris

NAN A. TALESE

Doubleday
New York
London
Toronto
Sydney
Auckland

PUBLISHED BY NAN A. TALESE
an imprint of Doubleday, a division of
Bantam Doubleday Dell Publishing Group, Inc.
666 Fifth Avenue, New York, New York 10103

DOUBLEDAY and the portrayal of an anchor
with a dolphin are trademarks of
Doubleday, a division of Bantam Doubleday Dell
Publishing Group, Inc.

Library of Congress Cataloging-in-Publication Data

Morris, Mary
A mother's love/Mary Morris.—1st ed.
p.   cm.
I. Title.
PS3563.O87445M68   1993
813'.54—dc20   92-25031
CIP

ISBN 0-385-42409-4
Copyright © 1993 by Mary Morris
All Rights Reserved
Printed in the United States of America
April 1993

3   5   7   9   10   8   6   4   2

To Larry, for everything

Acknowledgments

I would like to thank my friends John Harbison, Gerard Jacobs, Susan Eve Jahoda, Annette Williams Jaffee, Michael Kimmel, Varley O'Connor, Jodi Picoult, Mary Jane Roberts, Mark Rudman, Rena Shulsky, and my husband, Larry O'Connor, for all their insights during the writing of this book. Also my editor, Nan A. Talese, Jesse Cohen, Diane Marcus at Doubleday, Frances Apt for her scrupulous copy editing, and Amanda Urban, Marie Behan, and Sloan Harris at International Creative Management for all their support. And my parents, Sol and Rosalie Morris, for always being there.

A Mother's Love

ONE

BEFORE SHE LEFT, my mother used to practice her leaving on me. She'd say, "Come on. Let's go for a ride." "What about Sam?" I'd ask, for I always wanted my sister, Samantha, along. But Sam was not yet five, and my mother would drop her off at Dottie's trailer before heading with me into the desert. We'd get into the car and my mother would drive. She'd put the radio on High Desert Rock, roll down the windows, and sing all the way. Her raven hair was still long and straight then. I'd rest my head back, a girl of no more than seven, feeling the wind through my own dense red curls, wishing that I had my mother's thick, black hair.

After a while I'd just sit beside her in the passenger seat and stare at the desert, across the expanse of dust and sand. It was as if we were living on the edge of the moon and not in the state of

Nevada. The light moved across the contours of the arid red land and its beauty was otherworldly. At times it was a soft pink like a baby's flesh. At other times it appeared as if the world were on fire.

My mother would drive until she found a scenic place where she wanted to stop. She'd peer into the bottom of canyons and toss pebbles down the dark crevasses, counting the seconds until we heard the plop as they hit. Or she'd stand at the rim of the meteorite crater and gaze across its cavernous hole. The meteorite crater—that gaping scar a few hours from where we lived—was her favorite place to go. "Just think," she'd say, "some big stone came flying out of space and made this hole. Think of the power of the thing that did that." The meteorite itself had disintegrated when it struck. Scientists suspected that a piece of it was left in the southern slope, but no one had ever found it, though sometimes my mother dug with a stick as if she were looking.

She liked to walk the rim of the crater. She'd say, "You wait here, Ivy. It's too far for you," and she'd leave me sitting on a bench, the wind whipping my face until tears slipped from the corners of my eyes. She'd head out on the trail that meandered along the rocky ridge for some three miles. My mother wandered, her body growing smaller and smaller as she followed the sometimes treacherous path. If she wore a dress, the wind from the crater would get under the skirt, making it billow up as if it could carry her away like a spore. When she reached the other side, my now diminished mother would wave and wave. I'd wave back, motioning her to return; she seemed so small and insignificant there on the other side of the crater of that meteorite which upon impact had wiped out every form of life for miles and years to come.

It has been twenty-five years since I saw my mother on the lip of the meteorite crater. Or anywhere else, for that matter. Often I have thought of her leaving as if it were a story told to me by someone else. At other times I have wondered if my life hasn't shaped itself around this single event. Still, there were years when she hardly came to mind. But when I was pregnant with Bobby, my mother floated from the safe place where I had tucked her. As I lay awake during the darkened nights, she came back to haunt me.

I thought of her especially after Bobby was born when his cries woke me and I could not get back to sleep. Often he only wanted to be comforted, because he wasn't hungry or wet. It seemed as if he were afraid of something. I patted his back, rocked him. There, there, I said. It was what the nurse had taught me in the hospital. Pat him to calm him. Put him over your shoulder after he eats. Test his bath water with your elbow. I learned these lessons by rote the way, as a student,

I had once memorized the subjects I did not understand.

One night when Bobby was six weeks old, he woke with a start and it took a long time before I could get him settled down. Then I couldn't get back to sleep. I listened to sounds of people coming up the stairs—the would-be actress returning from her waitressing job, the bookie who managed the all-night coffee shop. I gazed out the window at the street below. The garbage had been picked through. Beneath my window lay chicken bones, a soiled Kotex, a pair of torn pajamas; on the sidewalk there was a lone shoe. The broken window across the street in the building where the drug dealers lived was boarded up now. Just the week before a naked man, blood streaming from his wrists, had stood in its smashed window frame, shouting, "Bruce! Bruce!" Christlike he'd stood, five stories up, while disembodied voices called, "Jump! Jump!"

Throwing open the window, I thrust my body outside. A cold breeze blew in. Craning my neck, I tried to look up. The city loomed, casting an eerie light on the clouds. If only I could see above the houses, I told myself. If only I could see the sky. I could hear Bobby breathing heavily in the middle of the unmade bed. Pulling myself back into the room, I put my face beside his. His skin smelled of talcum powder and perspiration. When he sweat, he smelled like a puppy. I pulled the cover across him, but he did not stir. We'd been like this for days, for weeks, it seemed, the two of us holed up as if we were on the lam. Running away. But in truth we weren't running. That is, no one was chasing us.

The room was littered with debris from the night before—containers of Kung Po chicken, Mandarin eggplant, bottles of beer, milk cartons. On a milk carton the face of a missing child stared at me. Since Bobby was born, I'd thought a lot about the missing, the vanished, the disappeared. The other day in a movie house where I'd gone for a matinee, until Bobby's cries sent me out of the theater, a mother and daughter sat down in front of me. They turned to each other in the dim-lit theater, heads bowed together as if in an embrace, silhouetted against the flickering screen.

My mother didn't leave all at once, though that was how it felt when my father snapped his fingers together, explaining to some acquaintance what had occurred. "Gone," he'd say, the click of his fingers piercing my ear. "Just like that." But I knew it wasn't a sudden leaving. It had happened over months and years—a rehearsed, choreographed event. My mother lived like an army on constant alert, prepared at any moment to take up arms, advance, evacuate. I knew this, but I never told my father. I always assumed she'd take me with her when she went.

Instead, she took my sister, Sam. I heard from them at first—a postcard from here and there—but I never saw them again. The postcards came from places like Sioux City, the Wisconsin Dells, or Idaho Falls, with no return address. She'd send a picture of a water slide, a dinosaur park. On them she'd scrawl absurd things about the landscape or what they were doing. On one she wrote, "They have great French fries here."

I've tried to remember the last time I saw them, but I have no memory of it. It could have been over breakfast or in the schoolyard. They could have been dressed in skirts or slacks. There was probably the usual flurry of activity—my mother's hurried kiss good-bye, a lunchbox pressed into my reluctant fist. In a sense it was as if my mother was always gone, so her physical departure didn't matter that much. She seemed to fade like a chalk image on the sidewalk after a rain, slowly washing away.

Though I do not remember the night my mother left, I remember things about that night. My father had driven in the evening for Lucky Cab—something he did to make ends meet—and I'd gone with him. After his shift, we walked home along Paradise Road, carrying coffee for him and doughnuts for me, laughing about something funny that had happened. A full moon cut a path across the desert as if it were really a road. The planet Mars was on an orbit that brought it closer to the earth than it had come in two hundred years. It shone overhead like a red, pulsating football. "You'll never see a night like this again," my father said as we paused.

Then we walked into our trailer on the outskirts of Vegas. The first thing we noticed was that it was clean, which was very rare. The dishes were washed, the beds made. The drawers and closets were neatly arranged, and half of everything they contained was gone. My father trembled as he moved from room to room, through the trailer looking for what was not there. Then he sank into a chair, his head buried forever, it seemed, in his hands.

It was after midnight as I sat at the window, drawing. I had tried to go back to sleep, but I only tossed and turned. So I sat at my work table, as I did many nights, while the baby slept. I drew sharp lines, the curve of a face. Coloring it over with an oil pastel, I drew it again and again, scratching at it with a fingernail. I built layer upon layer, coloring, scratching, drawing again, until the face seemed to come from somewhere deep within the image. Carefully I cut features—a nose, lips in profile—out of the clippings I kept in a basket. These I glued down, then brushed with oil paint.

Pausing, I looked outside. The plaintive sound of a saxophone came from the upper floors of the building where the drug dealers lived. It was dark in the ground-floor apartment of the old woman with the scrawny yellow Chihuahuas. Then she opened her refrigerator door, and I could see her naked body with its loose-fitting skin, dangling breasts. During the day she swaddled her dogs like babies in a confusion of rags and towels and rocked them in her window. Once in a store I saw numbers tattooed on her arm. Pablo's light was out, which was unusual, because he stayed up until all hours since his wife had died years ago. He too dressed his dogs and cat, only he had festive outfits for them—elf hats for Christmas, rabbit ears for Easter.

Then I noticed, walking up the street, the woman who lived across the way—the one who was about my age. She lived in the renovated building, next door to the drug dealers', that had gone co-op before any other on the block. Her apartment was directly across from mine, but one story up. It was late for her to be coming home, a sleeping child in her arms, another shuffling behind. Her hair was pulled back and she wore a black scarf around her head. With the child in her arms, too big to be carried really, she looked like a refugee in a war film. She had not always looked this way. For most of the six years I had lived in my building, I envied her all the things I thought she had.

Shortly after I'd first set up my work table at the window, the U-Haul van blocked traffic on the narrow West Side street. For an afternoon I listened to the blare of horns as she and her husband carried in their cinderblock bookcases, their old brass bed, the stained mattress that looked as if it had been stolen from a dormitory room. He was lean then and had more hair. She was pregnant with her first, who was now picked up by a school bus, but she was still tall and sleek. When her husband spoke to her, she laughed.

I have always done my artwork at the window —the jewelry I design and repair by the piece, which pays the bills. In recent years I have begun the paintings and collages of indeterminate faces. I work with things I find. I have drawers full, all neatly labeled. Souvenirs from motel gift shops— Oz memorabilia from Kansas, flamingos from Florida. Tickets, trivia, broken watches, instructions from an earthquake emergency kit, packets of Day-Glo stars. I create collages by building image upon image, sometimes cutting them out of newspapers or old postcards. Others I draw freehand. In my paintings concrete forms—roller skates, a tornado, a coffee cup—rise out of the abstract, but beneath the surface there is the face.

A few years ago I had a one-woman show and a critic called the face my "ghost face." He said the face, receding, elusive, was always the same. "Clearly," he wrote, "there is some story hidden here." After that review, I stared at my paintings, wondering whose it was, for it was not my mother, nor was it Sam. Before Bobby was born, I worked eight hours a day for the jewelry store in the diamond district, where the Hassidim, with mischievous glints in their eyes, come in, reaching into their pockets and pulling out fistfuls of gems. But on weekends, I painted my faces and watched the woman across the way.

When her first child was born, I knew because the delivery trucks brought the crib, the playpen. The old mattress was tossed into the street. A new futon arrived. She supervised the changes with the baby dangling in her arms, and I admired her energy and her verve. They got a white-and-black spaniel. She had her hair cropped short and he let his grow long. He began to wear jeans, except when the limo picked him up a few times a year, and then he wore a tuxedo, which made me think that he was in the entertainment industry—a producer of commercials or TV shorts—and had to go off to an awards banquet or important screening. Often she went with him. She'd wear slinky sequined gowns, strapless. (She wore the same midnight blue gown on several occasions.) I hardly ever saw her go anywhere else, unless it was to the store with a child in tow. A few times she went out with what appeared to be a manuscript tucked under her arm. Then she wore a skirt and blouse, and looked rather conventional. But when she got dressed up, when she tossed her head back to laugh, there was something glamorous about her.

A second child came, a boy this time. She grew pale and thin during the pregnancy, while her husband became rounder in the belly and balder on top. He began to smoke. She didn't laugh anymore when he talked. Now she planted flowers with a fury around the trees on the block and hammered up warning signs for dogs. In the morning she'd fling open the window and gaze down to check the flowers. The spaniel died and they got two new dogs—mutts that she never walked. They never ran or went to the park. She just took them to the curb, let them go to the bathroom right there, cleaned up after them, and took them back upstairs. The dogs, like her, were confined to the home.

When the little boy was toddling, she had her hair dyed an odd shade of gold, and I began to think something was wrong. She didn't want the second child. There was something else she wanted to do. A sadness that I'd sensed had always been there was no longer covered up with a smile. But soon her hair went back to normal. They put ski racks on the top of their car. She planted flowers around the trees the following spring. That summer they took their vacation as usual.

One day a few weeks before Bobby was born, as I worked at the window, her husband came to the door in a ponytail and jeans. He took a last puff from a cigarette and crushed it out with his heel, so I assumed she didn't know he was still smoking.

Then he rang their buzzer. He's forgotten his keys, I said to myself, surprised, because this had never happened before. She looked down with no expression on her face. A few moments later the children appeared, bundled in jackets, with small backpacks, ready to head out the door. He looked up at her, but she seemed unaware of his being there at all. He dropped his eyes to the sidewalk, shaking his head, and took each child by the hand, leading them away.

Since then, wondering how it was possible that I'd missed this, I have watched her more closely. Now she has a Russian wolfhound, a ridiculous brown thing. When she goes out with her children, she walks ahead of them. Once I heard her shout, "I've only got two hands!" It is just recently, as I've noticed her gazing in the direction of my window, that it has occurred to me that she has been watching me as well.

Bobby's cry startled me. While I was drawing, I'd almost forgotten he was there. Earlier I had nursed him in my bed, then left him there to sleep, thinking he wouldn't wake for hours. Now he had woken, but I wanted to finish what I was drawing, so I kept on, hoping he'd go back to sleep. His wail, though, grew more insistent. I pulled myself up from the chair and went over to the bed. He was shrieking as I touched his cheek, which was moist and warm but not feverish. Gently I lifted him.

He was soaked and the bed was too. Placing him on the changing table, I pulled off his wet pajamas, flinging them into the corner of the room where the laundry was piled high. I took off the diaper and hurled it into the trash. Bobby was screaming, his buttocks raw, his body exposed, cold, naked. His mouth opened into a widening gap, moving it like a suckerfish. As I rubbed cream on his genitals, his bottom, he quieted. His face looked soothed as I cooed and diapered him. He seemed to smile as I hummed a tune to calm him.

I tugged the urine-stained sheets off the bed and blotted the mattress. Holding Bobby to my chest, I went to the linen closet, but there was only one top sheet. I threw this on the bed as I patted the baby with my free hand. There, I said. It's all right. I put a dry washcloth on the wet spot and tucked in the sheet.

Then I lay down with Bobby, like a lover, in my arms. His skin fit against my skin like a graft. Resting him on a pillow, I let him nurse. As he drew milk, warmth raced through my body. It was a soothing tug that made Matthew seem even farther away than he was—across the bridge in Brooklyn. But now I drifted from the city as if I were traveling to a warm place—an island with tropical flowers, birds soaring. A seascape rose before me. Palms overhead. It switched to the desert, the place I've always known. Mojave. I felt myself walking across hot sand until my eyes closed and I slept.

I woke with a start. Bobby's head had slipped off my chest and was wedged between my body and the pillow. The nurse had warned me about pillows. I jerked up, thinking he'd suffocated. Gripping him, I pulled this creature of less than ten pounds back onto my chest. His breath rose and fell in rhythm with my own. His heart pounded against my heart, breath against my breath, and we stayed there through the night.

In the morning the sun shone, a clear blue winter's day. I made the bed. I pulled the single sheet tight along the edges, folded the blankets smoothly on top. Later I'd do the wash, the dishes, but for now at least I made the bed. It was a promise I'd made to myself. When my mother lived with us, there were unmade beds, dirty dishes stacked in the sink. In my dreams I saw her in a nightgown, the shades drawn, with ashtrays and cups of stale coffee surrounding her. I never remembered her dressed unless she had somewhere to go. My father says it was hardly ever like this. "Your mother was a very neat woman," he said once, defending her. "She always got dressed and she kept a nice house."

This may be so, but it is not what I recall.

TWO

KINGSTON CAVERNS was a full day's drive from Las Vegas, but once my mother took us there. I don't remember much about the long drive, except for the tarantulas that we crushed as they raced back and forth across the road and the fact that Sam was with us. It was the only time she went with me and my mother on our excursions. Sam wore a pair of blue-and-red overalls that were too big for her. She wore this same outfit the whole time we were away, so I assume my mother hadn't taken the time to pack.

With her red hair, the same color as mine, and her birthmark, Sam looked like Raggedy Ann. She had a strawberry mark, like a star, on the side of her face. It wasn't very big, but she kept her hand moving there as if it were a stain she could rub away. I liked to touch it, thinking it could warm my hand. After they were gone, I searched for

Sam's face in malls and airports. I knew this mark was the way I'd find them.

My mother hated the tarantulas with their furry bodies. She thought they were poisonous, so no matter how much I pleaded, she wouldn't stop and let me look at them. She wouldn't try to avoid them as they scuttled across the road. Little devils, she called them, creatures from hell. The crunch of their bodies punctuated our drive. It was dark when we reached the motel in a town where everything looked like the Old West, complete with wooden sidewalks, saloon, and hitching posts. There was the jail, the post office, the general store. But it was all fake. Just façades. We ate dinner that night in a cafeteria that served platters of fried chicken, which Sam and I devoured while our mother sipped black coffee.

In the morning she was in a hurry to get going. She told us to dress quickly, though Sam could barely dress herself. She looked at me helplessly as she fumbled with her buttons and tried to pull on her shoes. My father always dressed her, so I had to sit on the floor and tie her shoes while our mother stood impatiently at the door.

We took the winding road to the caverns. The road was bumpy as it rose through canyon country where the rocks were pink and green. I thought my mother would take us with her into the caves, but she pulled up in front of the cinderblock house where the woman who ran the caverns sold soda and postcards. The house had a room off to the side that served as the nursery and kennel. "It's too far for you girls to walk," she said. "I'll pick you up later."

The place smelled of urine, and there were anxious dogs with a desperate look in their eyes. The dogs, which could easily have roasted to death inside their cars, howled and whined in their cages. A partition separated the nursery from the kennel. In the nursery a few infants dozed. The only carpeting on the cool cement floor was a small circle with blocks on it.

"All right," my mother said, tapping us on the head. "I'll pick you up later." The woman, who was Hispanic, looked at us askance but said nothing. I believe we were too old for this facility.

"Now you girls behave," our mother said, waving good-bye. She looked very young and pretty in a white blouse and blue skirt, her black hair piled high on her head. "Do what the lady says."

"Don't worry," the woman said. "I'll take care of them. Enjoy yourself."

"I will," my mother said. "I will."

Sam whimpered and began to cry. She always was that kind of child, given to shifts of mood, sudden drops into despair. She was like our mother in this regard, laughing one moment, weeping the next, and I found myself annoyed with her. I was more like our father, carefree and fun-loving. At least I was until my mother left for good. But now I comforted Sam. I put my arms around her until she stopped crying. I held her to me and she sobbed into my chest.

The woman, who had pockmarked skin and greasy hair pulled back from her face, led us around by the hand. We spent the morning on the floor, playing with a block set. I built a city for Sam, complete with roads and buildings, places to hide and play, and eventually Sam picked up blocks and helped me. We built a series of tunnels where moles could live and a rocket ship to outer space. The woman listened to a Spanish radio station and read us a comic book. She gave us juice and oatmeal cookies for a snack. Then she had us lie down on clean white cots. Sam went right to sleep, exhausted from her efforts not to fall apart, but I told the woman I was not a napper. I had never been a napper, I insisted, a fact of which I was proud. So the woman rubbed my back until I fell asleep.

We woke to some excitement as a nervous couple arrived to deposit their infant, who cried and cried as his parents were leaving. The Hispanic woman kept waving them away. "He'll be fine. Soon as you're gone," she said, "he'll settle down." The mother, who was very young, kept looking back. The baby did settle down after his parents left, but it wasn't much later when the couple returned. The woman looked as if she had been crying. They took their child away.

After that the day just dragged on. We went with the woman to take the dogs for a walk. "I don't think we'll miss your mother if we go outside for a little while," she said, shaking her head. She clasped our hands and the dogs' leashes in one hand. The leashes left marks on our arms. There were three dogs—a large reddish-gold one and two little poodles. The big red one seemed to like Sam and me—because of our red hair, I reasoned —and he licked our faces and played with us. I hoped that its owner wouldn't come back and we'd get to keep it. But eventually we grew weary even of the red dog. Other couples came and went, collecting their sleeping infants. The woman kept looking at the clock and shaking her head. She had started to tidy up, perhaps wondering where to take us for the night, when our mother arrived.

She was flushed, and now her hair tumbled down her back. Now the woman rose in a huff and pointed to the sign overhead, which she read to my mother. It said something about taking your children if you plan to leave the premises.

"Oh," my mother said indignantly, "I did not leave the premises. I've been visiting the caverns all day. I've been fascinated by everything I saw." She began to talk about the bats that had flown by the millions from the mouth of the cave, about the green underwater pools and the colored columns of rock that stood upside down. She said she'd learned that a bat can locate its pups among a million bats, just by their voices. She described for us a strange, underground world, a maze of caves in which you could easily lose yourself. At first I felt certain that she had seen all those things.

But my mother was different then from the way she'd been earlier in the day. Even though there was something relaxed and soothing about her, she wouldn't look Sam or me in the eye. Her blouse was wrinkled and the collar was smudged; she didn't have any lipstick on. I could tell she'd had a good time. I also had the feeling she hadn't spent the day by herself.

When we got outside it was dark, and I wanted to ask her more about the caverns, especially the bats she'd seen fly from the mouth of the cave, but something made me think better of it, and I said nothing at all. "So, you girls must be hungry," she said, almost as an afterthought. "Do you want to go for dinner somewhere?"

We went to a diner, where Sam and I ordered hamburgers. My mother picked French fries off our plates, carefully dipping just the ends into catsup. She hardly ever ate. She said it was for her figure. She drank black coffee and smoked cigarettes and sucked oranges. During a meal, she'd nibble off someone else's plate. After dinner, we drove until my mother said she was too tired to drive any more. We checked into a dingy motel on Route 66. Almost all my mother's excursions were along Route 66. She liked this highway because, she said, it could take you anywhere—wherever you wanted to be. The Mother Road, it was called. She used to joke about that.

Just before we went to sleep, I said to her, "Don't you think we should phone Dad? Let him know we're all right?" She looked at me in an exasperated way and I knew I'd failed some test I didn't know I was taking. That night Sam and I slept in the same bed, and she wrapped her arms and legs around me as if she were a monkey clinging to a branch. Often at home Sam would crawl into bed beside me, though I tried to kick her away. She'd hold on, no matter what I did to pry her loose. But in that motel room I let her cling to me as tightly as she ever had, and did not pry her away.

It was late the next day when we arrived back at the Valley of Fire trailer park. My father sat in a lawn chair on the porch, cigarette dangling from his mouth, a drink in a tall amber-colored glass clutched in his fist. He rushed to us when he saw the car. "Oh, thank God!" he cried, pressing me and Sam to him. "Thank God you're home."

I don't know how many nights later it was when I woke to find my mother standing in the doorway of my room. The light from the bathroom shone behind her and I could see the curve of her hips, the outline of her form. She was naked and trembling. My mother had a trim, sleek body with breasts that were sturdy and taut, and she often walked around the house naked. She seemed very strong physically, though she did nothing to stay in shape. But now she shook like a frightened rabbit. "Oh, Ivy," I heard her say, leaning her body against the doorjamb, "I had a bad dream."

"What did you dream about?" I asked. Her long black hair was disheveled. She was waiting for me to invite her in. Sam, who slept in the bed next to mine, stirred slightly. I was happy to be the elder, to have my mother confiding in me. She came in, pushing my legs aside, and sat down on the bed.

"Oh, I don't want to tell you. It was about my early life." I knew little about my mother's past, and what I did would come after she was gone, from my father, though his past was also vague. It seemed then as if my parents had come from nowhere, and later, when I learned about spontaneous generation in school, I thought they had sprouted from the soil.

Now she began to weep. Dropping her head, she sank onto the pillow beside me. I didn't know what to do. I put my arms around her and she nestled into them. Her flesh was soft and smooth, and she smelled of perfume and liquor, cigarettes and soap.

"No matter what happens, promise me, Ivy, promise me," she said, "that you'll be a big girl. You'll be strong."

"What's going to happen?" I asked.

"Nothing. I don't know." She clasped my hands. "You know what I hope? I hope that when you're grown up, we can be friends. We can take walks and talk about everything that's happened to us."

Tears welled up in her eyes and she pulled me to her. Her breath was warm against my face; her nipples pressed into my chest. I stroked my hair. I don't know how much later it was that my mother fell asleep and I sat up beside her, hovering the way I'd once seen a dog in a movie beside his dead master, not letting anyone near.

THREE

PATRICIA CAMPBELL sat at her kitchen counter, making gazpacho in a blender and Heloise's boric acid roach balls in a bowl. "That looks good," I said, pointing to the roach balls as I walked in. She handed me the recipe. Sugar, flour, bacon fat, onions, boric acid.

"The roaches love them," Patricia said as she mashed the mix, stuffed it into small aluminum-foil boats, and tucked them into drawers. "I haven't seen you for a while." She tossed her blond hair off her face with the back of her hand. She stood tall, regal, like a figurehead on the prow of a ship.

"Well, it's not so easy for me to get downtown these days," I said with a laugh, pushing the stroller into a corner and dropping Bobby's bag, filled with his bottles, diapers, change of clothes. I rubbed my shoulder where the bag had been.

Patricia reached for an armful of wet clothes and tossed them into the dryer. She dropped another load into the washer. I glanced into her living room: magazines were neatly stacked in corners, the books were in alphabetical order. When she opened the refrigerator, it sparkled with fresh fruit and vegetables. The roaches were a part of life in New York (the neighbor's roaches, really, Patricia said), but everything else was clean, white. I thought of the dishes I'd left in the sink, the pile of newspapers by the door. The cartons of take-out food in the fridge that I dipped into for dinner. "Some days," I said, "I don't even get outside."

"I can imagine," Patricia said, making me wonder if she could. "I'm overworked too. It's not that easy to get together anymore." Patricia and I used to see each other almost every week. We'd meet somewhere midway for a quick dinner or a six o'clock film. But since Bobby was born, she had come uptown only twice—once to the hospital and another time shortly after I brought him home. Though we spoke often, we hadn't seen each other in several weeks.

She'd gotten home late and was rushing to fix dinner. Brown rice was already cooking, and she grabbed some carrots and broccoli, slicing and dropping them into a steamer. When she took out two white fish fillets, my heart sank. I was so hungry these days. I had to eat frugally to save money. Still, I was eating, but it seemed I could never get enough. Even though I hardly ate—and couldn't afford—red meat, I had been hoping for steak, lamb chops, something to fill me up. Instead, I munched on the cheese and crackers, and sipped the seltzer Patricia had placed before me.

She moved quickly through the motions of salting the fish. She hadn't had time to change after work, and she still wore a skirt and sneakers. Patricia was one of those women who walk home as if they are on military drill. "I'm always late," she complained. "The city brings me down. I'm always in a hurry, but where am I going?"

"It's true," I agreed. "I used to feel that way too, that I didn't know where I was going. But now, well, I think I know." Bobby began to whimper and I tried to distract him with a rattle, but he cried in earnest and my milk started to flow. He stared at me, angry at being denied, through his black eyes—his father's eyes. It was difficult for me to look at him and not think of Matthew, though I tried not to. In some ways it might have been easier if I'd had a girl. I could not bathe Bobby or change him—I could not look at his naked body—and not think about the man who fathered him.

Tentatively I picked him up, undoing my blouse. Bobby moved his head up and down as he struggled to reach my breast. "I wish you'd come to see us more," I said to Patricia.

"Oh, I try, but you know. Everyone's so busy.

Our lives are so demanding." I nodded, then frowned. Bobby clamped down, his mouth firmly on my breast. Lately I didn't seem to be so busy anymore.

Patricia saw me wince. "It hurts?"

"A lot," I said. "They just don't put it in any of the books."

Patricia nodded as she set the table, sorting through the knives and forks. Patricia had nice things. She had real silverware and porcelain plates. She had silver spoons for ladeling gravy and soups. She had things that had belonged to her family. Antique furniture from her aunt's farmhouse. Her bed was the one her grandmother was born in. When she married Scott, her mother had given her the family linen, the chest that had held her own trousseau. On her dresser were pictures of large groups of people—the extended family—taken at their annual reunions. In some a yacht was moored in the background, waves lapped a Maine shore. Other reunions were held on the family farm, the one they still owned upstate. It had a name. Shady Creek. "This weekend," Patricia would say, "we're going to Shady Creek."

I'd met Patricia, who was now a reporter for "Crime Time" ("Crime Time on Prime Time," the promotions read), in my condo conversion class when I was getting a real-estate agent's license. "Look where we'd be now," Patricia liked to say as we watched the market bottom out. She enjoyed her job in television. She had tried various things, such as real estate, catering, and now "Crime Time," where she was a researcher. She called up police officers and asked them what their favorite crime was that week, and they always told her because they weren't fools and they wanted to be on television just like everybody else.

Patricia liked to call me with the horror story of the week. She said that Americans couldn't get enough of horror. Children stuffed in plastic bags, old women bludgeoned to death for their makeup kits, retarded people locked in closets for years. It wasn't sex, she liked to say, that gives America its kicks. It's blood, terror, the unthinkable crimes. "Americans love dismemberment, especially if it comes in sequence," Patricia told me once over a cup of tea. Serial crime and mutilation; those were the biggest things. Randomness helped. Perhaps, I mused, because we lead such fragmentary lives.

Once she had tried to work out a segment based on me. She had stared at the picture I keep on my dresser in a small silver frame, the one of me and Sam at Lake Meade the year before she disappeared. Two little girls in bathing suits, arms locked around each other. "You never know, your sister might see it. Mysteries have been solved this way." But the producers balked. It wasn't exactly a crime and it had happened too long ago.

"So what are you working on now?" I asked

innocently as Bobby quieted down. I stroked his black hair.

She grimaced. "You don't want to know."

I shrugged. "Tell me."

"Organ theft," she said.

"What?" This was something I had not heard of before.

"Oh, it's a big thing. A man goes into a bar, orders a beer. A beautiful woman sits down beside him. Soon he leaves with her. Three days later he wakes up in pain in a warehouse on a slab. He makes his way to a hospital and finds out that one of his kidneys has been surgically removed."

I shook my head. "This isn't possible."

"But it is." Patricia smiled; something about her relished these stories. "A kidney is worth ten thousand dollars. It's capitalism," she said, "supply and demand. People will pay good money." She paused, gauging my reaction. I stared at her, incredulous, shaking my head. "There are worse stories, but I don't want to upset you."

"Like what?"

She gazed at Bobby. "Oh, children in some places in the world"—she spoke hesitantly—"are being sold . . . for spare parts." I could feel the look of horror spread across my face. "But think of it, Ivy. If Bobby needed a kidney, a liver, eyes, what would you do? Wouldn't you buy them if you could? No questions asked?"

Patricia was infertile. She had reached that conclusion well before her doctors, who continued to probe, dig, test for compatibility. Like a patient with a terminal illness, she paid their bills, begrudging them every dime. "I waited too long," she said. She had just turned thirty-eight; she'd been trying since she was thirty-five. Patricia was one of those women who were born to be mothers. She kept a birthday calendar tacked to her bulletin board. She always knew just what gift to buy. An occasion never passed without her sending a card. Phone calls to her never went unanswered. She was on top of her life. Except that something had happened—a form of infertility for which there is no discernible medical cause—and she and Scott were unable to conceive.

Patricia had spent years having her womb swept, her tubes blown open like paper straws, her blood and urine put through every cycle like a stubborn stain in the wash. Scott had splayed himself on the paper-covered doctor's tables and ejaculated endlessly into cups as if he were a prize bull, his seed spun like cotton candy, enriched, juiced up, and injected into his wife as if to help Patricia produce some new, healthier strain of life.

She had taken pills that sent her into paroxysms of grief, others that made her lethargic as a sleeping bear. Twice she and Scott had tried "the gift," at eight thousand dollars a try—all of which had failed. She had endured the humiliation of having her orifices probed, scraped until the doctors declared they could find nothing wrong. But when she still did not conceive, she had consulted a Chinese herbalist—a man of few words who worked in a musty room, surrounded by aging apothecary jars, who plucked her hairs, testing them in vials of acid—and told her to stop all previous medications, who made her drink a brew of grasses and twigs, dried petals, iguana bones, deer antlers, all ground fine and boiled into a steamy, sickening broth.

So while Patricia sat up night after night, insomniac and alone, drinking the bitter brew that made her shape her arms into hopeful cradles and would leave her as fallow and solitary as before, I had conceived a child on the one and only night I had ever, on a drunken whim, been careless with Matthew, who had been my lover on and off for years; we had a tacit agreement that marriage and children were not a part of our carefully shaped pact with the world. It seemed as if this child had come to me the way the Trobriand Islanders believe—not through intercourse, which serves only to prepare the way, but rather as a spirit that swims to you while you are standing, receptive, in clear water.

"I envy you," Patricia said. "You've always known what you've wanted." She stared at Bobby. "And you've managed to get it."

I shrugged, wondering how she could think this was the case when I felt as if things had been thrust upon me. "I don't think that's true," I said, pulling Bobby to me. "I think my life has been one long accident." If this had been another century, a different world, I might have handed my baby over to Patricia. What was I doing with a child on my own? It made no sense, really, certainly no practical sense.

"You have a lot, Ivy. You should consider yourself lucky." Her voice was bitter.

"I have almost no income," I said, taking Bobby off my breast. "I have no one in my life."

"You have your work," she said, "and you have your child. You might make a living from your art someday."

This was a big *might*. Already I couldn't figure out how I was going to make ends meet. It was when I began trying to be an artist and money was tight that I had gotten my real-estate broker's license. I had taken such courses as "Rentals, from the Ground Up," and "Know Your Client," and "Condo Conversion." Patricia and I had sat in the back of drab classrooms, listening to teachers drone on about how to put a family of four in a two bedroom with a walk-in closet and call it a three bedroom. How to convince someone who is elderly or frail that a four-story walk-up is good exercise. On my first sale a woman bought a basement apartment because I convinced her that the garden brought in a lot of light. She called me a year later and said she'd actually thought about killing me.

I took people in and out of other people's lives. Sometimes the people moving out were on the up and up—new marriage, new child, a better job. They were in search of bigger space, a new way of living. But more often than not it was those in life's difficult transitions I saw—the ones whose marriages were breaking up, who'd lost their jobs, the people growing old and weak, the had-to-sells, the must-leaves. From cheery yuppie couples in leather coats who clutched bundles of joy or who were expectant, brimming with life—people who couldn't imagine anything going wrong any more than a healthy person can imagine illness—I moved into lives plagued with death, divorce, and financial ruin.

One day an old woman who was moving from her house of forty years into a retirement home in Queens took me by the hand. She wept as we made our way through every nook and cranny of her house. "This is where my husband read the newspaper. This is where my sonny used to play," the one who was putting her in the home. She spoke as if everything had just happened, but it was all decades ago.

"Even if I starve," I told Matthew, "I'm done with this business." Patricia had not lasted very long either.

She refilled my glass. "Do you have a beer?" I asked.

"Sorry." She shook her head. "We've given up drinking. The herbalist's orders."

I smiled, sipping my seltzer, wishing it were a beer. She dumped more crackers and cheese cubes onto the platter before me. "You look tired," she said.

"I'm exhausted," I confessed.

"I hear it's a lot of work."

"It's more than that," I said, shifting Bobby again as I ate. "It's a lot of work for two people, let alone one."

Patricia sat beside me, staring at the baby. "Would you like me to hold him," she asked tentatively, "so you can eat?" Her hands trembled as she reached for the baby. I was relieved to hand her my child.

"Here," I said, "take him." She took him into her arms and held him in front of her as if he were glass, as if she might drop him and he'd break. Balancing him on her hands, she seemed amazed at how light he was, yet when I carried him for hours and hours, his weight grew in my arms. She pulled him to her, cradled him, and he moved his mouth to nurse. Patricia seemed to know instinctively what the nurse had had to teach me. She cooed, she smiled. His eyes lit up.

Before Bobby was born, Patricia told me that she used to sit up at night, drinking her third or fourth Chinese herbalist's brew, using biofeedback to create in her mind the image of her child as a psychological researcher had taught her to do. Imagine the child in your womb, he'd said. Try to picture it. Try to feel what it is like to be expecting a child. He had sketched on her stomach with a black marker that would be difficult to remove the silhouette of a baby, and she was supposed to sit for hours and contemplate, literally, her navel.

As she cuddled Bobby, talking to him, I pitied her for having had this denied her, yet how could I tell her I wasn't even sure I wanted it myself? She had never given him a present. She'd said, "I want to find just the right thing," but she hadn't found it. She had stopped talking about it and I hadn't asked.

Now she took a sip from the herbalist's brew. He had added a twig, she told me. It makes the outside of the ovary soft as the shell of dying turtles. It was supposed to make the egg shoot out like a rocket. Hard ovaries, that's what the herbalist said. Petrified eggs. You must be an old soul.

Patricia had argued with Scott about adoption. She'd told him, "I'd love whoever they put in my hands." But then she'd read an account that said babies from foreign countries were stolen. Mothers in Salvador, Guatemala, were arriving with legal claims. Romanian children were being ripped off. As with spare parts, this too was big business. The brokering of children. There was that woman from Guadalajara who spent five years searching for the son she ultimately won, breaking the adoptive mother's heart. Patricia wanted none of it.

"So," she said, letting Bobby rest precariously in her lap, "I think we'll work out our life differently. We're going to buy a house in the country with the money we've been saving for day care, that sort of thing. You know, we'll fix it up."

"That sounds like a good idea," I said, "but I don't think you should give up."

"Well"—Patricia sighed—"it's been years. We've done what we can . . . And Matthew?" she asked, switching the conversation over to me. "What about Matthew?"

We were trading grief for grief. Matthew hadn't wanted the baby; he'd made that clear from the start. Though he was only slightly older than I, he had a boy who was almost grown. "A mistake from my youth," he called him. Ricky was the product of Matthew's one and only marriage, to a Venezuelan dancer, a woman named Serena. Ricky was the color of a cocoa bean and read backward. Everything he wrote was backward. Once I'd helped him with his homework, and I could see him struggling to turn it all around.

"Kids," Matthew had said to me after that visit, "they're more trouble than they're worth." When I told him I was pregnant, he'd said, "Don't worry. I'll be there for you." Meaning for the abortion. I had never intended to have this child, but when I went to the doctor, he put a stethoscope to my womb. I heard the sound of a heart, no bigger than a bird's, resounding like a sonic boom. When I told Matthew I was going to have the child, he moved whatever belongings he had in my place back to his studio in Brooklyn. We hadn't seen each other since just after Bobby was born.

"I talk to him," I said, "but I don't see much change. He doesn't seem to want the responsibility."

"No money?"

"Some," I lied.

"Are you managing? Are you getting by?"

I took a deep breath, feeling my stomach tighten in knots. "Oh, sure we're managing. What choice do we have?"

Patricia looked at me hard now and I knew what she was thinking. That life wasn't fair. That she should have my baby and then my lover would come back to me. "Nothing is perfect," I said.

She nodded. "I suppose nothing is." She handed Bobby back to me, her face flushed, her hands shaking as I extended my arms to take him.

FOUR

IT WAS LATE as I made my way to the subway, pushing Bobby while he slept. Although I'd promised Patricia to take a cab, it would have cost at least five dollars, maybe more like seven, to go uptown. The night was cold and miserable. A wet mist covered the city. The wind was penetrating, damp. A homeless man dragged a green plastic bag of tin cans that rose behind him like a helium balloon. A woman with matted black hair, stinking in her own urine, talked to her shopping cart. An old woman dressed as a baby sat in a doorway, sucking on a bottle. Panhandlers approached and receded into shadows, sensing that I was not good pickings. A garbage can was on fire. Nobody stopped.

"I'm going to call Matthew and tell him to come and get us," I said to no one in particular. A woman turned and gave me a worried look. I smiled, pretending to be conversing with the baby; I had seen women with small children muttering to themselves before. Bobby squirmed in the cold, yet sweat covered his brow. What if he were ill? What would I do then?

I wondered what would happen if I took Bobby right now to Matthew's studio. If we just showed up, he would have to let us in. It was weeks since we'd spoken, and I felt a longing settle in. What was he doing now? Was he listening to his favorite jazz station the way he liked to do in the evening? Was he alone? I didn't want to think about that. At least he'd see the baby he'd seen only once before. Maybe he'd even offer me some money so that I wouldn't have to ask. In front of me a bedraggled man shouted into a cellular phone as he staggered across Sixth Avenue, dodging oncoming traffic. I hailed a cab, but when the driver saw the stroller, he drove off. I walked to the IRT.

Reaching the stairs, I wrapped my hands around the stroller and heaved it into the air. Slowly, one step at a time, I made my way down. An uptown express pulled in, but I was only on the first landing. "Hold the train!" I shouted, but no one heard. I dragged the stroller down each step, the baby bouncing inside. My arms ached. My hands were raw. From the platform I saw a disposable diaper lying on the third rail.

The local pulled in, packed with night travelers. Wall Street brokers coming home late, theatergoers, couples, crazy people, homeless people, single people. People who looked as if they got dressed and went to work every day of their lives. A small space was grudgingly made for the stroller and me. Then someone offered me a seat, and I collapsed into it.

A large black man in a green workshirt and green pants, who appeared to be coming home from a long shift, sat across from me. He stared with watery, bloodshot eyes and I looked away. I closed my eyes, though I was afraid that if I fell asleep, I'd miss my stop. I looked up as we arrived at Sixty-sixth Street. Now the train was less crowded, but the black man was still sitting across from me, his eyes on me and on the stroller. I thought I might still get off this train and go to Matthew's studio.

The studio was in an industrial part of Brooklyn—the far reaches of the F or D train—and when I was pregnant, I used to go to there unannounced. It was in a neighborhood of meatpackers and auto parts, of lumberyards and junkyards. Huge warehouses and abandoned factories. There was a prison not far from the studio, and at night I could see the hands of men clutching the bars. The city's detritus seemed to lie along the avenues, which were ugly in a way that made life seem empty and pointless. I felt endangered even if I wasn't, and I didn't like to go there.

When Matthew first rented the studio, I went to

help him set it up. He was a photographer who had gained some success with his images of America. He had done three series—Rednecks, Cults, and Halls of Fame—that had earned him some acclaim. Once, when I had my first painting accepted for a show, I showed up with a bottle of champagne, but he seemed displeased. After that I couldn't bring myself to go again. But in the months before Bobby was born, as I watched Matthew float in and out of my life, a disappearing act, I found myself going back. I went whether he asked me or not, and he didn't seem to care. Still, it was not something I wanted to do, but he came back less and less to the apartment we'd shared.

The last time I went was when I was four months pregnant. It was a muggy September night, and he made dinner—a summer salad, poached salmon, orange juice spritzers. Matthew was an excellent cook; he did all the cooking when we were together. He cooked and I cleaned up. The best meal he ever made was when we were staying in a cabin in Maine, the night we conceived this child. We bought vegetables at a farmstand and two bottles of wine. We caught rainbow trout in the river outside our cabin. Then we sat under the stars, eating the crispy fried trout, drinking. All night long I could smell the fire and taste the trout. Even now I can taste it.

After dinner the night in his studio before Bobby was born, Matthew said he wanted to take a walk for some ice cream. So we walked down a street that stank of garbage, excrement, decayed meat. The air was thick and yellow, and I felt as if I couldn't breathe. "I'm not sure how to say this," he stammered after we bought the ice cream and were heading home. "Maybe I've already said it. I love you and I want to stay with you, but I can't be father to this child."

"You'll feel different after it's born," I said.

"Maybe I will and maybe I won't, but, Ivy, I'm already feeling different about you." He paused, taking a deep breath. "You should have ended it . . . when you had the chance."

"Maybe," I said, "but I didn't."

"You mean you couldn't."

"That's right. I couldn't."

"And why couldn't you?"

I shook my head. "I don't know," I said. And at the time, I didn't.

"Have you thought"—he paused again, choosing his words carefully—"how you'll manage?"

It was the first time I realized he wouldn't be with me. With us. I began to ponder the tasks I'd have to do for myself. Morning coffee, food shopping, the cooking. When we were together, Matthew took care of those things. And then of course there was the baby, the money, the long nights. "I'll manage," I said.

When we got back to the studio, we were hot and sticky, and I felt heavy and tired. For a moment I stood in front of the industrial-size air conditioner, which did not cool the entire loft, and let it blow on me. When I stepped away, I was still hot. I knew I had to leave, but I kept hoping he would ask me to stay. I went to stand behind him and run my hands through his hair. He had beautiful hair, thick silvery curls, like an aging Botticelli angel. When friends saw us side by side, me with my flaming red and Matthew with his cool silver locks, they called us "fire and ice." "I'm going," I said. "I think it's for the best." Still I let my hands run through curls. "Do you want me to cut your hair?" I asked, whispering into his ear.

Matthew prided himself on the fact that he had never been to a barber. Only women cut Matthew's hair. It was a vestige of his youth. His mother had always seemed complacent and sober, "almost normal," Matthew said, when she cut his hair. After his mother came Serena, then the girlfriend before me, and now me. "Yes," he said, kissing my hands, "I'd like that." So he sat in the chair, towel draped around his neck, while I snipped, letting the silken hair tumble to the floor. Matthew was the first man who looked at a painting of mine and said, "This is good," who fed me when I was hungry, who took care of me. I wanted to gather his hair, keep it in a Ziploc bag in the back of a drawer.

When I was done, he turned ever so gently and reached for me. He pressed his face to my belly, running his hands up and down my swollen breasts. "Are you sore?" he asked. "Am I hurting you?"

He pulled me to him, thrusting my head back and kissing me. His tongue searched deep within my mouth, and I didn't pull away as he tugged at my T-shirt, my bra. Without turning on the light, he led me into the bedroom, where he pulled off my clothes and his and made love to me slowly, letting me come over and over again. Then he thrust himself into me, hard, not so slowly, and I pulled back, recoiled. "I want you," he said, "I really want you."

He thrust himself deeper. Our bodies stuck with sweat as he pushed himself deeper and deeper, straining, I could tell, so that he would not come. I watched him pushing, his face grimacing in the moonlight, and I saw that this was not the face I had known. I shoved him away. "Are you crazy," I said. "What are you trying to do?"

But he held me down and thrust faster and harder, even as I struggled and tightened beneath him as if I were protecting my child. At last he came, a solitary, lonely ejaculation, as I tried to move him off me and away. He fell, weeping, into my arms. "I can't help myself," he said, his body heaving against mine.

I ran my fingers through his silver curls. "I know," I muttered, wanting to get away. "I can't help myself either."

At 103rd I almost missed my stop. Grabbing the stroller, I raced off the train. It was nearly midnight, and the platform was deserted. The stench of urine sickened me and I held my breath. Bobby woke and shrieked, hungry. I patted him and pushed on, and he quieted with the motion of the stroller. As I traversed the platform, I heard noises behind me, heavy footsteps on the cement.

Turning, I saw the black man who had been staring at me on the train, now walking behind. I picked up my pace, but so did he. I was almost at the turnstile and he was about twenty feet behind. If I could just make it out, I'd be all right, but he was gaining. I pushed through the iron gate, turned to the stairs. Before me were about thirty steps and behind me was the man and we were the only people in that subway station. As I bent down to pick up the stroller, I felt his body bending over mine. I looked up into his red eyes. He was sweating and perhaps he had been drinking. I don't have anything, I wanted to say.

I stared at my sleeping child. I'll snatch him, I thought, then dash up the stairs. "Lady," the man said softly, "can I give you a hand?"

Tears rose in my eyes. "Yes," I said, "I suppose I could use a hand."

With a grunt, he hoisted the stroller into the air and carted Bobby, whose head bounced up and down, to the top of the stairs. The man was straining, breathing heavily, until he put the stroller down on the sidewalk. "Are you all right now?" he asked me gently. "Can you make it from here?"

"Yes," I said. "I can make it from here."

"Okay, then. Well, you take it easy. Good night."

"Good night!" I shouted. "Thank you!" But he was already gone, disappearing into the shadows of the night, the stranger whose intentions I had misconstrued. Miserable and ashamed, I made my way home. At last I reached my door. I stood in front of the brownstone and saw that no lights were on. Everyone slept. I stared at the darkened house. There was no one to go to. It was late and cold.

I carried the buggy up the stoop and into the entranceway. I didn't have the strength to carry it further. I pushed it into a corner and hoped that no one would steal it in the night. Scooping Bobby into my arms, I carried him. Together, we climbed the stairs. After fumbling for the keys, I finally walked in and stood in the darkness, catching my breath. Then I turned on the light.

It was late as I nursed Bobby and lay down beside him. I was just falling asleep when the phone rang. The ringing pierced the quiet. "Hello," I said, hoping it was Matthew on the other end. Perhaps he too was having a change of heart. I still slept on the side of the bed where I'd slept when we were together, our bodies curled up like a pair of sixes—a lucky number, I always said. Sometimes I reached, thinking I'd find him stretched out there. He still had a set of keys. "Hello." But I heard the crackling of long distance —the sound of mountains, rivers, empty terrain. "Who is it?" I said, and then, "Is that you?"

It seemed to be more than just a wrong number, because the person on the other end paused, as if wanting to hear my voice. So I asked, just as the phone went dead, "Mother?" as if this were suddenly possible. "Is that you?"

The phone call had awakened Bobby, and I could not get him back to sleep. He cried and cried and would not be comforted. "Please," I said to him, "don't." I paced, carrying him in my arms, but he wouldn't stop. "What is it?" I pleaded. "What do you want?"

I sat down at my work table, cradling Bobby as he screamed in my arms. I should have been working on the free-lance jewelry settings Mike had sent over—priceless diamond earrings that, if I'd hocked them, would have paid all my bills for months, an inlaid pendant that was out of style, a ring that was being reset for someone's fiftieth wedding anniversary—but I pushed them aside. Balancing Bobby on my shoulder and trying to rock him, I shuffled through my postcard collection. I'd been mulling over an idea for a long time —a ghost face in a desert scene at night, ensconced

· 47 ·

in images I would copy from my postcards. The World's Biggest Apple, the Dinodiner, the Corn Palace, a Vermont cow. I arranged the postcards on the work table as best I could next to a preliminary sketch for the face. The composition had eluded me, but now I saw how the face could fit slightly off center, encircled by some of these images, as if it were rising out of the hills.

Now that it was clear, I wanted to draw it, but Bobby would not stop crying. Perhaps he was exhausted, overtired from the trip downtown. Or hungry, but for what I could not tell, because I had nursed him before he slept. Maybe he was just frightened and upset at being awakened. Whatever it was, he would not settle down. Suddenly I found myself trembling with rage, and I had to put him in his crib. He would have to cry himself back to sleep. A few days before in a New York hospital a child was found in a lavatory, a note pinned to her jacket. "Please take care of my child. I don't want to hurt her." I could see what had made the woman do that.

I went back to my work table, listening as Bobby's cries diminished. Picking up a pencil, I tapped it on the table. But instead of drawing, I began to map out a budget. Periodically I made a list of expenses—$550 for rent, $50 a week for food and diapers, $50 a month for phone. (When I called my father, it was collect.) As it was, we were just getting by. I had no idea where the money for a baby sitter would come from so I could go back to work. I couldn't think about clothes for Bobby when he outgrew his newborn things.

With a sigh, I put the pencil down and stared out the window. The light was on in the apartment of the woman across the way. It was a small light in the living room, but she didn't usually leave her lights on, so I assumed she too was unable to sleep. She was upset. I could feel it, wishing there was something I could do.

Even though I didn't know her and we had never spoken or even said a casual hello, I felt as if I knew who she was and what had happened to her. I knew the plot of her life. What had brought her to this place. Even how she felt about it. It was a clarity that shocked me, an inevitability that surprised me. It was as if I had written the first word on a page, drawn the first line on a canvas, and the other words and images followed, of necessity.

I remember my own early life the way you remember a clearing in the woods that you passed at dawn, only to return in the late afternoon when the light shines on it in a different way—the movement of the light altering its surface—so that you're not certain whether it's the same clearing, the same woods. It looks familiar. But you can never be sure. So it is with my life.

What is memory to me but a story I have told over and over, embellishing it each time, making it better or worse, depending on the listener. It never comes out the same way twice, and now I am not even sure of what really happened, for I have lost the line between what occurred and what I have made up. In this sense I have come to resemble the woman across the way. It occurs to me at times—and my father says this is so—that I have remembered my past all wrong. Once I read a study that said that creative people tend to recall their childhood as unhappy experiences, no matter how filled with tenderness and love they may have been.

My father says that everything was fine until I was seven years old and my mother, Jessica Hope Holmes Slovak, went crazy, as her own mother had. She was twenty when she had me, twenty-seven when she left. It was in her genes, my father said, which hardly made me feel better, since I share those genes. When she left, America was poised for change. Soon Kennedy would be elected —and assassinated—the Beatles would sing on "The Ed Sullivan Show," and flower children would arrive in the Haight. But already my mother believed she wasn't leading the life she was meant to lead. In a sense she was ahead of her time.

The light of the woman across the way shone in the darkness and I sat, transfixed by its glow. Even the drug dealers had gone to sleep. At last Bobby grew quiet and soon settled into sleep. I breathed a sigh of relief as I gazed outside. Perhaps a phone call had also awakened her. A child had a bad dream. Now a silhouette passed through the room. Suddenly the light went out, the room went black. There was a poignancy to this, the thought of her alone in the dark, struggling to go back to sleep.

FIVE

THE GLASS SLIPPER, where my father worked, was on the Strip. Children weren't allowed, but once my mother dragged us there. She drove in our beat-up Dodge from the Valley of Fire trailer park and parked it beside all the fancy Mercedeses with the California plates. She wore tight gray slacks, a cigarette dangling from her mouth. Her long black hair was pulled back in a ponytail.

My mother clasped our hands in hers, almost pulling Sam off the ground. Red welts swelled on my wrists, and Sam cried, "You're hurting me," until she loosened her grip. Whenever she was angry, I saw it in her eyes. They were dark but shiny, like two pieces of coal just plucked from a mine, and her face went stark white, all the color draining from her lips. Her tongue, which was always moving in her mouth, moved ferociously now, yet her eyes were set straight ahead like a ferret's on its prey.

The Glass Slipper was made almost entirely of glass before such buildings were fashionable. It was shaped like a shoe, and we took an elevator in its heel straight to the Cinderella Lounge, where my mother hid us behind her as she gulped down a rum and Coke. Then she took us by the hand again into the casino, where my father dealt blackjack. She stormed up to the table and didn't seem to care that people were standing around. My father wore a neatly pressed white shirt and a bow tie. He had on red suspenders, and his coppery hair was combed flat to the side. For a moment I didn't recognize him. I just thought he was a handsome man.

As she pulled us to where he stood, my father's face went pale. "Howard, I cannot take it anymore." She raised our fists into the air. "I simply cannot take it."

People playing at my father's table slipped away. He gazed nervously around for his pit boss, then motioned for a standby to fill in. Putting his hand on my mother's shoulder, he took her off to a corner, where they seemed to forget about us. "Jessie," I heard him say, his hand gripping her arm. She stared at him, her features all pinched together. Even when she was angry she was the most beautiful woman he could have found. But there was something strange about her features. With her black hair, her white skin, and red lips, she never looked quite real. It was as if she were a Disney character, someone somebody had drawn.

"I cannot stand it," she said emphatically.

Their voices faded, and I could only see their mouths moving. There was something in my father's face that made me know he was begging. They had forgotten we were there, I had forgotten about Sam. When I looked for her, she was gone. I looked everywhere, and then I saw her, standing in front of the bank of elevators, a little girl in a thin cotton dress. When the elevator opened, she got in. "Sam!" I shouted. "Don't do that!" But my voice was drowned out in the din of the casino, the whirling of wheels, the sound of chips dropping into palms. The doors closed and she was gone.

My parents must have looked my way and seen me frantically pounding on the elevator doors. My father dashed across the casino and began banging on the buttons. He was desperate, hitting at the elevators with his fists. "Why didn't you watch her?" my mother shouted at me. "Why did you let her go?" as if I were responsible.

Suddenly the elevator returned. Its doors opened and there, standing alone and bewildered, was Sam, tears sliding down her cheeks. My mother grabbed her, clutching her in her arms. She reached for me as well. "I'm sorry, Ivy," she said, "I don't know what gets into me. I'm sorry." My father put his arms around all of us and for a moment we were entangled in one another's arms. Then he kissed my mother hard, letting his lips linger. "Wait up for me, all right?"

She smiled, nodding, looking as if she were falling asleep. "I will."

She drove us back in silence to the trailer park. We drove down the rows of trailers, some with real yards and even trees in front, which made them look like homes. My father had bought our trailer for a thousand dollars from a former dealer who had moved to Arizona when his wife died. Many of the people who worked in Vegas and serviced the casinos lived in trailer parks on the outskirts of town, and my father had friends nearby, nice people who had kids. They liked to drop in and have a beer, though my mother did not approve of them and never offered them lemonade or "something a little stronger," the way my father did. Our trailer had a porch with green outdoor carpeting and a barbecue. The windows on the side had green awnings to keep out the extreme heat. There were lounge chairs out front and a small yard where we could play.

Inside the trailer was another matter. Everything had a layer of grime or was falling apart. Things needed fixing. When we lived in California, my mother seemed to take care of the house. But once we reached Vegas, it all stopped as if she had gone on strike. Whatever it was, she had no interest, as other mothers seemed to have. Sometimes Dottie, who lived next door, would wash our clothes for school or bring us a casserole for dinner. When Dottie came over, my mother perked up. Together they washed the dishes, straightened the house. Then they sat on the porch and smoked cigarettes and drank lemonade. My mother seemed happiest at those times, and sometimes she'd even call me to her and give me a hug for no reason at all.

When we got home that evening, my mother paused in the kitchen to rinse out a glass so that she could pour herself a drink. The water streamed over the sinkful of dishes that were washed only when we needed them. Sometimes Sam and I would wash them, but this was just for fun. My mother sat down with her drink on the lopsided sofa in the dark and dreary living room. She fiddled with the antenna of the black and white TV, but she couldn't get a picture, so she gave up. She tapped her fingers on the table that held the lava lamp with its blue-and-gold undulating glob that my father loved and his collection of knickknacks—miniature glass horses, cats, odd things like that. When she got up, she went into their room, which was off the kitchen. She took her drink with her and she closed the door. We didn't dare disturb her when she did this.

I could hear the bed creak as she lay down. The only piece of furniture in their room, other than a reading lamp (though I don't recall ever seeing anyone read), was the bed, which seemed to consume the room. I wondered how it had gotten in there at all, and it seemed to me to pose the same problem as a boat in a bottle. My parents' dresser had to be in the living room; often they walked naked to get their clothes. My mother never actually made the bed. If she bothered at all, she threw the covers together so that it was a series of lumps, giving the impression that someone or something was asleep in it. I got into the habit of being quiet whenever I passed their room for fear of waking whatever might be sleeping there.

Though we had not had our dinner yet, I took Sam into our room. It was always a mess, with clothes and toys strewn everywhere. I'm sure that in the years we lived there nobody bothered to pick anything up. Instead of playing, Sam and I sat quietly on my bed, listening. A little while later my mother came out with a glow on her cheeks, dressed in a sheer pink gown. "That's good," she said, seeing us in our room. "Now I want you girls to hop straight into bed."

She must have forgotten that we hadn't had supper, because she made us get into our pajamas and brush our teeth. I think it was more of an oversight than malice, but often we went to bed with an empty, hungry feeling inside. This night she put Sam right to bed, though Sam protested and whimpered. She told me to go to sleep as well, but when she saw me staring at her from the door of my room, she said, "Come here, Ivy. Talk to me." So I went to her.

"What do you want to talk about, Mom?"

"Oh, I don't know. I just hate not having someone to keep me company. Tell me about something." So I told her about the math test I'd taken that day—how I'd gotten all the addition right, but hadn't done so well with the subtraction. "Oh," she said. She banged a cigarette on the windowsill and lit it. Her face illumined like a Halloween mask, the lines deep around her eyes. "And who did you play with?"

I began to tell her that I'd played at recess with Anna, who also lived in Valley of Fire trailer park, but that Anna's brother was sick—he was always sick—and she had to go home early. My mother didn't ask me anything about my test or Anna's brother. She hummed songs from *South Pacific* while she stared out the window.

"If only we could go back to California," she said. This is what they fought about mostly. "If we could go back to the sea, everything," she said, "would be all right." Actually we'd never lived by the sea, though to my mother I suppose we had. My father used to fold the laundry while my mother sat, dreamily contemplating the career she would have had in California. What she wanted more than anything was to be discovered. But my father refused to return to where everything, she swore, would happen for her.

"Ivy," my mother said. She liked to say my name; it was the name she'd given me. A fitting one, she used to say, for one who likes to cling. My father had wanted to call me something old-fashioned, like Emma or Sarah Jane. He never liked Ivy; he called me Lucky Red because of my hair and because when he gambled he claimed I brought him luck, like a rabbit's foot or a shiny penny found by the side of the road. He said he did better when I was there. "Ivy," she said again. A car passed and she perked up, but it drove on, its lights reflecting on the stop sign across the street. She pressed me to her as if she would crush my bones. "We'll go home."

Before moving to Vegas, we'd lived in a valley of smog in a trailer park, near San Bernardino, called the Desert Sands. Where we lived, it was verdant, but across the street, just on the other side of the road, the desert stretched before us, dusty and dry. We could have lived closer to the shore and to the hardware store on Melrose where my father carved the keys for the would-be actors, the wealthy ladies of society, the has-beens, and, on rare occasions, the stars, but he preferred the dry, inland air.

My father worked in the back of a small appliance shop as a maker of keys, which he ground until the fine metal dust settled into his lungs, leaving him asthmatic and wheezing for the rest of his days. He unlocked doors and repaired locks for people who lived in houses we could never imagine, and he'd come home with tales like the sailor back from the sea. He'd say how he'd made a key for a man who had white tigers roaming in his yard, or he'd changed a lock for a woman whose swimming pool had an underwater cave where tropical fish swam. When my father told us these stories—most of which I am certain he made up—he'd get a distant look in his eyes and the next day he'd take me into the dark, smoky bars with card rooms hidden behind closed doors or down to the bannered track, where I watched the prancing thoroughbreds in the paddock while he gambled our life away. It was his hobby, he told me, the way he liked to spend his time.

On Saturdays he would take me to the track. He'd stand by the paddock and study the horses as they paraded by. He watched their hooves and their mouths. He'd study the racing sheet and place his bets. For me, the track was one long wait. I never much enjoyed the time between races. My father would find his cronies, slumped over beers and the racing page. "Here," he said, "look at this one, good on the turf, but not used to five and a half furlongs. He brought his own jockey down." They'd congregate in the bar while I stared at the muddy track, furrowed with hoof prints.

When the bartender wasn't looking, my father took me with him into the bar, where the "boys," as he called the aging men with potbellies, would tease me. "So, Lucky Red, who're you betting on in the seventh?" I'd bet on impulse if I liked the sound of a name. Dream Feathers to win, Time Flies to place. They laughed when I told them my favorites—these men who weighed each hot tip, studied their forms. But I seemed to win as often as they did.

The trumpet sounded and the horses headed into the paddock. My father kept me near him, his lucky charm, and I was happy being close to him. He chewed on his pencil or on a cigar and pointed to the horse that was going to win. Then they'd go to the gate. I liked the frisky ones that kicked and tossed their heads. When the bell went off, and we heard the pounding of hooves, he would clasp my hand, raising it higher and higher as the horses rounded the home stretch.

Sometimes we won, but mostly we lost, which I liked better. Because then my father took the colored betting tickets—those tickets in orange and blue and yellow and red, those tickets which came in a million colors—and he'd tear them into confetti, sprinkling them on my thick red hair. We'd drive home with the windows down, my hair filled with the confetti of losers' tickets that fluttered around the car like snow.

When I was five, my father gave in to his passion. He packed us up and moved us to Nevada, where legal gambling became what he did with his life. His dream was to become a partner in some business venture in Vegas. Real estate or the hotel industry. He said, "You'll see, it's the future of America. Right there in the desert." My mother didn't believe him. To her, Nevada was just a desert, recently turned nuclear test site. But he believed—and he was right—that Vegas would see a big boom and its values soar. On moving to Vegas, he said, he would do things right. He made a promise that he would give up gambling, and during the time she lived with us, he kept his promise. Only once did he break it—when the Lions Club put three tons of ice in front of the Golden Nugget and took dollar bets on when it would melt.

The night we drove east along Route 66 into the cold desert, Sam and I huddled in the back under a scratchy blanket, our mother complaining the entire way. It was the first time I'd traveled on that road, but I knew it was the one my father had taken to come west. There was a moon, but nothing else to see, and I kept thinking that he was taking us to a place where we'd lose ourselves forever. I thought that the sound of coyotes, the sudden rise of hawks, the dry desert sand were all I'd ever know. That my life would be jackrabbits and tumbleweed and nothing more.

It was late when a set of headlights pulled up at last in front of our trailer. I don't know how long I'd been sitting at the window in my mother's clasp, but I felt as if I'd been holding my breath for a long time. Even though she'd said she wanted to talk, we had hardly spoken. Once or twice we'd blown our breath on the glass and written our names in its fog, but that was all. Now she loosened her grip as my father got out of the car and slammed the door. He glanced toward the trailer, looking first dejected, then eager as my mother waved. We both waved at him, but she patted me on the rear. "Go to sleep now, Ivy; go to bed." But I wanted to stay where I was, nestled against her by the window, and then fly with her into my father's arms.

As I slipped away from her body, I was surprised by how cold the night had turned. The floor beneath my feet was like ice and my empty stomach gnawed at me. The door opened and I heard my father come in. They went toward their room, arm in arm, the light from the room illuminating the space between their arms, a small space you could slip coins through. They talked for a while in the low voices that you use when telling secrets. Then their light went out and they were quiet, except for the rustle of sheets, the creak of the bed.

Later I woke to the sound of someone moving through the trailer and I knew it was she. My mother was a restless sleeper. Often I would hear her prowling at night, rummaging through things as if she were a raccoon. I listened to her moving about for a long time, wondering what she was looking for, until I drifted back to sleep.

It was early when Sam woke me, whimpering for food. She shook me, asking me to find her something to eat. "I want peanut butter," she said. She shook so hard, she rattled the bed, even as I tried to push her away. Though it seemed as if Sam was always trying to stuff things into her mouth, she was a skinny child with tiny bones. Yet now she rocked me with all her might.

I crept out of bed, wondering what I'd fix for her and for me. Sam slipped her hand through mine. The light was dim in the trailer as I opened the refrigerator door, on which my mother kept a list of chores, her menu for the week. She tried to do things to maintain the semblance of a normal life. The menu for the five nights of the week was always the same—meatloaf, boiled ham, roast chicken, noodle casserole, fried fish. But we never ate those things. I have no memory of eating roast chicken on Wednesday or any other day of the week. But I remember the list, because I was always hungry for the food my mother never made.

Sam wanted peanut butter and jelly but I couldn't get the top off the peach preserve. I tried, but it was useless. So I opened the door to our parents' room. The room was dark with the shade drawn but I could make out my mother, lying on her back, her black hair sprawled across the bed. My father moved on top of her, whispering over and over her name. They were bathed in sweat, glistening like sardines.

SIX

DINNERSTEIN & SONS, Jewelers, was nice enough in the front, its rows of cases filled with mostly diamond and pearl settings. But in the back where I worked it was little better than a sweatshop, lit with bare fluorescent bulbs. A dreary place. It was here that settings were replaced, stones reset. I was skilled at this, and Mike, the owner, paid me well. It was much more than he paid his two stringers, Alma and Suzette, who resented me because I worked free-lance and came and went as I pleased.

I worked at a bench like them, though they did only pearls. All day long they sorted through the bins, picking out the best freshwater or cultivated variety. The rosy pearls, the grays and blues, the pure whites. It was tedious, unappreciated work. Alma, a black woman in her forties who'd raised two boys alone, read gothic novels on her breaks and had tiny stuffed bears all around her desk. Suzette, who came from Normandy and hated America (I had no idea why she stayed, but I think it had to do with a man), did her nails in her spare time, grinding them with a file. Alma had the eye for the right pearls, but she had been doing this for a dozen years. Suzette was better with the sizing and stringing, so they divided their tasks along these lines. Alma often accused Suzette, behind her back, of being color blind when it came to picking out the right pearl.

Alma and Suzette had basically ignored me for years until Mike, a stout man with a bulldog face, came into the workroom shortly after I'd told him I was pregnant and said I should go ahead and make myself a ring—pick out any diamond I wanted. "A present," he said, "from me." The "girls" raised their heads.

"There's not going to be a wedding," I told him.

Mike shrugged, embarrassed. "Well, if there's anything I can do."

"Keep me employed," I said. "I'm going to need it."

After Bobby was born, the office sent me a silver teething ring and cup, engraved. I was grateful for these gifts, but I could have used more practical things, though Alma did send a pair of pajamas. Suzette, who was not a mother, gave him a pair of tiny white silk shoes.

The day I returned was the first time anyone,

except Mike, who'd stopped by the hospital, had seen the baby. Ben, who worked in the front, handed him a lollipop, which I intercepted. "Thanks, Ben. He'll eat it next year," I told him. Since Bobby was born, I'd been doing work by the piece at home when I wasn't working on my collages. But now I needed to earn more, so I decided to return a few days a week. I hadn't thought through how I'd manage. Eventually I'd have to hire a baby sitter, but for the moment the baby could sit on the bench beside me in his Kangarockaroo.

"Oh, he is cute. You'll never regret it," Alma said in a voice that made me unsure.

Suzette stopped filing her nails long enough to glance up. "Nice baby," she said, looking incredibly bored.

I sat at my workbench, where three diamond rings and one pin setting awaited me. This was a full day's work, at least, if I went straight through. I began with the pin because it would take the most time. It was an heirloom, missing a few of its precious stones. There was a note attached, saying that this was Mrs. Potter's mother's brooch and that it was important that the piece be done properly. I pictured Mrs. Potter's mother at the turn of the century, wearing this brooch on her bodice. A Victorian sitting room, apricot damask curtains.

For the first hour Bobby slept as I cleaned the setting. I scraped and polished. I had earned my living for years as a jeweler and designer, specializing in silver and gold. Gold illuminated my youth or at least colored the tales my father told of the casinos where he worked with carpets spun of gold, of a desk where all the knobs were silver dollars and the phone solid gold. Of the Golden Nugget and the legendary Golden Lady, who dressed in gold—gold skirts, gold boots, her skin tanned a perfect tawny shade of gold, her hair shimmering like golden fleece.

I have held various jobs, some better than others. I've been a photographer's model, for though I'm not beautiful, I am striking, with my thick red curls. At times I think I might just as well be a college professor or a legal secretary, a computer technician or a veterinarian. I did many things, but nothing really held me. Perhaps my peripatetic youth—so much moving around, my mother's leaving—made my concentration poor; my mind tended to wander from the tasks at hand.

But I was drawn to tiny polished objects, to perfectly carved pieces, to bits of silver and gold. My stepmother, Dottie, our former neighbor, first noticed I had talent. "A gift," she called it. Though her notion of art was the velvet painting from Tijuana of a tiger or the crying clowns that graced her living room, Dottie watched me doodling, sketching what I saw. I liked to take an object apart with my eyes. But what impressed her the most was that I drew things that weren't there.

People, animals, landscapes. Whatever was in my head. I could close my eyes and see animals I'd only seen in books—like giraffes or angel fish—and these I'd draw in amazing detail. I could sketch the Eiffel Tower or Elvis crooning on TV. I also did odd sketches of my desert world—a scorpion, its tail raised to strike; a coyote sleeping in its lair. Sometimes I drew my mother's face, pressed against a window, looking out into nothing at all. Or a woman with a girl like Sam buying purses in a store. Dottie would discreetly admire these. One day, she told my father, "She has talent, Howard. I'm going to see that she gets to use it." It was Dottie who pushed me to take a class at the local community college when we were still living in Vegas and later saw to it that I went to art school in Los Angeles.

When I can, I do my work at home, then bring it in to Mike. In the front room of my apartment —the only room that's sunny—I have Ziploc bags tucked away with diamonds, emeralds, sapphires, as well as less precious stones like tiger's eye and turquoise, purple onyx and mother of pearl. Occasionally museums send me pieces that their own conservators can't repair, and I am well paid for this work, though it doesn't come in often enough. Once I spent a year on a necklace worn by an Egyptian queen who had died three thousand years before. On my table I had hundreds of the glass beads and pieces of gold chain. I was six months into the project when Matthew bumped into the table, and it took us weeks, during which we could not vacuum, until we found every single colored bead.

I was a little more than an hour into the heirloom brooch when Bobby awoke. I sighed at being interrupted, and Alma raised her eyes. She made room for Bobby on the bench so that I could change his diaper. Suzette, a disgusted look in her face, turned away. It would take almost half an hour to feed him, and if I wanted to get the work done, I didn't have that time to spare. I found a cushion, propped him on it, and let him nurse while I worked. Alma shook her head as I struggled not to drop him. When he was done, he was awake and wanted to be held.

"Here," Alma said, "I can take a break. You work. Come here, Bobby, play with your Aunt Alma for a while."

I've always liked Alma. She too was the daughter of a long-departed mother. Once I shared my past with her after work over drinks, confiding my secret. And Alma said, "I don't know what makes white people think this is so special. It happens to blacks all the time." Half her friends, she said, had mothers who went away or didn't know who their fathers were. "You want to know the definition of confusion? Father's Day in Harlem." She tossed back her head of plaited curls and roared.

Alma played with Bobby until her break was over. Then she smiled at Suzette. "Suzie, honey," Alma said, "why don't you entertain the baby for a while?" Taking pity on me, perhaps, Suzette put down her nail file and shook a rattle in his face during her break.

Halfway through the day my stomach growled. I hadn't had breakfast and it was almost lunch-time, but I didn't want to spend money on a mid-town sandwich. I should have brought something from home, not that I had much in the fridge. My stomach growled again, and I thought that lately I had the gnawing emptiness that I had not felt since my mother forgot to give Sam and me sup-per before bed. Alma looked over as I smiled an embarrassed smile. "Ivy, have you eaten? You've got to eat something."

"I'm okay. I don't want to stop."

"But maybe you *should* stop." She had half a tuna fish sandwich and a cup of coffee on her desk. "Here. Take these . . . if you don't want to go out."

"No, really, I'll be fine," but she shoved the food over to my workbench. I took little bites, but I felt ashamed. When I was done, it was as if I hadn't eaten at all.

We divided the day, taking care of Bobby until Alma and Suzette had to go, leaving me at the bench, where I worked until past seven o'clock. I was growing weak with hunger, but I kept working. When I got home, I'd make something to eat.

It was going to take me almost ten hours to complete a job that normally took six. As Alma was leaving, she'd said, "Ivy, let me give you a piece of advice. You can't do this on your own. You have to hire somebody. And you need to take care of yourself." I nodded; she was right and I would get someone to help, though I knew it would be weeks before I could afford it.

When I was getting ready to leave, Mike, who was doing the books, handed me an envelope with cash for my day's efforts. Two hundred dollars. "This is too much," I said.

"You worked ten hours; that's what you get."

"Mike, half the time I wasn't working. It was a six-hour job and you know it. I can't take this money."

"Take the money; you need it."

"I'll take pay for six hours' work and not a penny more."

Annoyed with me, Mike took fifty dollars out of the envelope. "I'll put this in my desk. It's there if you need it."

"Thanks," I said, tears filling my eyes.

Exhausted and ravenous when I reached home at eight o'clock, I looked in the refrigerator and found some eggs, butter, a few slices of bread. While I heated a skillet, I put Bobby in front of the television; "Nature" was on with a show about hummingbirds. He seemed transfixed by the luminous colors, the beating of wings. As I cracked three eggs into the skillet, I heard the narrator explain that the female hummingbird raises her young alone and alters her body functions in order to do so. Her pulse increases, her body temperature drops to conserve strength. Some females, the narrator went on, die of exhaustion, in which case the chicks starve.

I put my eggs on a plate and began to eat greedily, paying no attention to my son. Perhaps I could devise a way to drop my temperature, raise my pulse. I ate as if I were truly starved; I couldn't get the food into me fast enough. It was a while before I noticed the stench, still longer before I paid attention to it. Maybe it wasn't the smell but Bobby's cry that got my attention. And then it took me longer still to see what was wrong. As I bent over him, I saw that his clothes were soaked, drenched in light brown liquid that oozed out onto his shirt, covering him.

I picked him up and saw that he was soiled everywhere. Even his baby seat. I had to find a way to rinse the filth off him. A bath wouldn't work because the dirt would fill his tub. And besides, where could I put him while I got the tub ready. I could take a shower, holding him in the shower, but all I wanted to do was eat.

It occurred to me that I could rinse him off in

the sink under the faucet. Then I could wrap him in a towel while I finished eating. Later I'd bathe him properly and dress him for bed. Peeling off his soiled clothes, I tossed them aside and ran the water in the sink, equal amounts of hot and cold. Balancing him in my hand, I let the water rush over his body, and rubbed a little soap on him. "Now that feels good, doesn't it?" I said. He seemed happy to be washed and to feel the water coursing over his body. He cooed as I swished the water over his chest, his legs, his genitals; the filth that covered him was whisked away.

Perhaps because I was tired and hungry, because I could not think, I stood holding Bobby under the faucet, wondering how I could turn the water off and still hold the baby. I seemed incapable of just letting the water run while I got the towel and wrapped him up. So, clasping Bobby firmly in one hand, I turned off one of the faucets with the other. Suddenly his face turned red, then shaped itself into a howl of pain. It took only an instant before an actual sound was uttered and I grasped what I'd done. I had turned off the cold water, leaving the hot to flow over my child. I stared into Bobby's gaping mouth. It was the first time I had seen him in pain, let alone pain that I had brought upon him. I pulled him away from the hot water.

His face was red and wrinkled as he screamed,

like an old man's. I held him up to the light. He was not burned, but he screamed and screamed. I have scalded my child, I thought, crushing him to me. I am like her, I said, and this proves it. I am just like her.

SEVEN

M Y MOTHER sat at the door of the trailer, sketching—something she liked to do. She sketched mountains, valleys, the clouds, the scene from the window of our trailer. Even as a child, I knew her drawing wasn't very good, but she didn't seem to care. Neither did I. I sat watching her for a long time. As she drew, her tongue moved in her mouth like a lizard's. It was always strange to me that when my mother wasn't talking or eating, her tongue kept moving, twisting, flicking.

I used to watch the lizards on the rocks near our trailer, and I saw how their tongues flicked even when they had no insect to grab. The connection between my mother and lizards fascinated me and I began to think about these cold-blooded creatures—their nocturnal habits, their love of warm rocks, the swiftness of their movements when danger was near. But none of this gave me any clues to understanding my mother. It just seemed as if they both flicked their tongues even when they had nothing to land on. Nervous tongues with nothing to do.

That day my mother must have grown impatient with me hovering at her side. "Here," she said, motioning, "you can take some colors." She had a box of crayons with forty-eight colors in them, something I had coveted for a long time. "You can draw."

I drew a pink sun. A blue cow. "Oh, no, not like that," she said. "That's not right. I'll show you how."

"I know," I said. "I can do this." I drew a purple chimpanzee, rainbow rocks, bushes that burned red.

"That's not right," she said. "The colors are wrong."

"I like it this way," I replied.

"You think you know everything, don't you? You think you know it all." I was six years old and I stood there, crayons clutched between my fingers, but she grabbed them from me. "Well, that's not right, that's not how you draw." And she broke the crayons I'd been using, every single one.

A week later she bought me my own box of crayons, but it had only sixteen colors. This was her way of apologizing. "Here, now we don't have to share," she said. "Now you can draw with these." I stared into the box, then stared at hers, for she had bought a new one for herself, the same big box with the forty-eight colors. She gave me the box of sixteen, but it wasn't like hers. There was no silver, no flesh, no gold.

EIGHT

I BEGAN MY SEARCH again. Periodically over the years I have searched for them. Hired detectives, run ads. I knew it would be useless. Even if I found them, what would I discover? Still, I began again. What is the point of looking for someone who left of her own free will? Who had been gone so long? What did I hope to find? But how could I expect to be a mother without finding my own mother? The two became inextricably linked in my mind; it seemed impossible that I could be the former without finding the latter.

I read somewhere that a person spends two years of his or her life searching for things—objects misplaced. Receipts, a screwdriver, the missing mate to a sock. The everyday searches that make up our lives. In the end we devote two solid years to such banal quests. In my case I wondered each time I looked for my mother and Sam what the numbers would be. Ten times that? Or more?

I found myself staring at the faces of the missing on the post office bulletin board. Children snatched from supermarkets, an elderly woman who left on a snowy night. I used to read the tabloids, thinking a familiar face might appear. I began again to read whatever I could get my hands on—clippings from newspapers, articles Patricia sent. Some simply amused me, such as the sweet Polish couple who took off with their savings and their children's inheritance to live it up in the islands for their last years. Others—like the story of the woman who every year since 1973 on her daughter's birthday took out a classified ad in dozens of newspapers across the land, "Barbara, happy birthday, darling, please, come home"—moved me to tears.

I pored over accounts of reunion, of untold joy. The man who located his boys after a search of nine years. The Chinese mother who'd never stopped looking until the daughter, stolen from her at birth, was found. The one that intrigued me the most—the one I carried in my wallet for years —was about the missing sea captain. His ship had arrived back in port in Baton Rouge without the skipper on board. The authorities as well as his crewmen were perplexed. He was too happy to have killed himself. He was popular and unlikely to have been pushed. He was too good a sailor to fall into the sea. There was a possibility that he had taken off on his own. One wet suit was missing. But he had been a doting father, a loving husband. He had only a $37,000 life insurance policy. Fraud was ruled out. To this day his case remains unsolved.

I know something about finding a missing person. You start with a name. Take my mother's name, for instance, Jessica Hope Holmes Slovak. You take all the parts of the name and you turn them around. Or you take grandmother's maiden name (Anderson in my case). This is the strange truth about people who are missing of their own free will: it is difficult to leave yourself behind. It is not that you can't change your name, say, from Jessica Hope Holmes Slovak to Angelina Fallachino, move to the middle of South Carolina where you know no one, invent a coherent history for yourself (born in Portland, Oregon, of Italian-American parents who were killed in a car crash). It is just not what people tend to do.

What they are likely to do is hold on to a piece of the past. They move back to a town where they once lived. (One man searched the nation for his wife and daughter for seven years, only to run into them in the produce aisle of the supermarket near his house.) They create a name that has a part of their previous name. They get in touch with just one person they once knew. Eventually they'll need to register a car, enroll in school, take out insurance. So perhaps my mother became Hope Anderson, moved to a part of California where we used to live. This is the likely scenario, because most people have neither the courage nor the imagination to reinvent themselves completely.

Patricia helped me get new lists of detectives who might handle cases like mine. Missing persons, abandoned children, runaways. I am comfortable in the world of detectives, for it is not so different from that of gamblers, with its seedy side, its smoke-filled rooms. Men living on the underside. I call and say I'm trying to trace my mother and sister, and the detective will dutifully take down all the information, fill in the missing person's report.

We breeze through the "last seen where" and "what is your relationship to the missing person." Then they get to the "how long have they been missing," and there is always a palpable pause. The more professional detective refrains from saying, "You've got to be kidding," but a few have said that, and worse. One said, "This is a joke, right?" Twenty-five years. It feels like a joke, except of course it is my life.

Sometimes the detectives are nice and say things like, "Lady, I'm not sure I can help you much with this." One even said, "Listen, let me give you a piece of advice. Get on with your life." I'm going to have a child, I explain, and this child has a grandmother and an aunt out there, and maybe they're even looking for me.

Just before Bobby was born I took my meager

savings and hired a man named O'Malley. An ex-Marine, he worked out of a second-floor office on the Lower East Side, the kind of office you'd see in those 1940s' cult films. Name painted in black letters on the frosted glass door; Peggy, the secretary, who wore bright red lipstick and nail polish. No pictures on the wall; paint chipping; papers piled everywhere. O'Malley was huge, with watery blue eyes. Peggy handed me a cup of instant coffee with Dairy Creamer when I sat down. I don't know if Peggy did this with everyone, but she looked at me with sad round eyes.

O'Malley specialized in marital cases. His office was riddled with evidence and clues—envelopes labeled "Strictly Personal," photographs, gloves. "More men hire detectives than women," he told me right away. "It's not often that I get a woman. Maybe women expect men to cheat." Male pride, he said; that's what kept his business going.

He'd done a murder case or two, your usual missing person, custody. "You know, one guy took off with his two little girls. That was six years ago. The mother hasn't been the same since. Can you imagine?"

O'Malley called Peggy over as I handed him a picture of a five-year-old girl. "Isn't that what you need?" I asked. "The distinguishing mark." He looked at the picture of the girl squinting in a bathing suit, and saw what appeared to be a shadow on one side of her face. "That's her birthmark," I said, "a strawberry mark. It can't be removed, not even with a laser. It's in the pigment. You can find someone who looks like that, can't you?"

I hired him at a cost that was dear, and he searched. He went to California and filed endless expense reports. He went to plastic surgeons and sent me lists of women who had tried to have such birthmarks removed. He actually found a California-based poet of a certain renown who matched the description of Sam, but her happily married parents lived in Nebraska, in the same town where they'd always lived. They were relatively confused by their daughter's literary success and thought the detective was from the press.

O'Malley called me after this and said, "Listen, lady, give it up. I know people who can't answer the phone or open a door or go to the mail and not think this is it. The letter I've been waiting for. The unexpected return. I know people, good people, nice upstanding individuals, who've made themselves sick."

After spending hundreds of dollars, I agreed that O'Malley was right, and I dispensed with his services. The day I let him go, Peggy took me aside, her coffee breath close to my face. "Don't give up," she said. "They're out there somewhere." When I phoned to tell my father, he was enraged. "You're going to need a baby sitter," he shouted.

"So you hire a detective. Does that make any sense?"

No, of course it didn't. But I could not help myself. How, I kept thinking, can I be a mother if I do not know my own mother? And the way to my mother was obviously through Sam. As I told O'Malley the day I decided to terminate his services, "You know, one day I'll walk into a mall, a crowded theater, an airport, and there she'll be. I'll see her. If it's going to happen, it will be like that." And O'Malley, a nice man, really, with a family of his own, nodded as he showed me to the door.

The nights are longest. Until the child learns to sleep, I imagine a thousand or more like this. Nights awake, that come out whole. Or tumbling into hard slumber, only to be awakened by a child's cries. What sleep there is comes in snatches —an hour here and there. A pause in the endless fabric that makes up my nights as a mother alone. So often I find myself gazing into space, peering into the apartment of the woman with the number tattooed on her arm who swaddles her Chihuahuas day and night. Or of Pablo, with his costumed pets. Or, of course, of the woman across the way. I follow her comings and goings; I detect her moods. I can tell now when her ex-husband is coming for a visit, because her face grows tense and she is impatient with her kids.

Often I bring Bobby into bed with me. I bring

him so that I can nurse and hold him and sleep, my life having reduced itself to the primordial needs. How long will I keep this up? Until he is three or six? Until people start to talk? It is at night when Bobby wakes me and I am lying in bed nursing him that I imagine what my mother's life and Sam's were like after they left. Did they wander around? Or did they just go to a trailer park on the Pacific Palisades and stay put? I have this image of my mother dragging Sam around from mall to mall.

My mother loved to shop; she loved to pick her way through piles of sales items. But her favorites were accessories. Costume jewelry, blue kid gloves. "You can dress anything up or down with a scarf," she'd say. And she'd buy whatever she could afford—things she'd never wear in the middle of the Mojave Desert. When my mother left, the only thing she didn't take were the drawers of accessories—the things she couldn't carry that we never knew she had. Snakeskin belts, alligator bags, elegant silk scarves with painted birds or tropical flowers on them. My father divided these between Dottie and me. I have enough accessories for a lifetime.

Once she gave me thirty dollars and told me to go shopping. "Pick out something nice," she said. "Something for yourself." I rode my bike to the mall and bought purple shorts, a blue top. I bought a pale green shirtwaist dress with a white ruffled bodice. When I got home, my mother said, "Let's see them." Nervously I tried on the shorts, the top, the dress. Her tongue clicked as she shook her head with each item. "No," she said, "these just aren't you." We took them back and my mother got a thirty-dollar store credit, which she tucked into her purse.

Probably she is still well dressed, living in a California bungalow with a small lawn, close to the sea, where she always wanted to be. She's had a few face lifts, but her body's in great shape. Still single, no one in her life. There hasn't been for a long time. Not much of a change, really. But for Sam I see different things. A subdivision near the sea called the Ocean Breeze or Mediterranean Shores in a town like Laguna or Newport Beach. She has had some new technology laser surgery on her birthmark so that it looks as if she's got a touch of sunburn on one side of her face. I wouldn't recognize her anymore. She's got a husband who's a junior executive for Database, two kids.

They belong to Temple of God, the one where women fly across the cathedral dome, dressed as angels in gossamer gowns. Perhaps she has been convinced that her father was an evil man who led a dissolute life and I was the dark one, just like him. I used to think—and my father had this checked out—that my mother had whisked Sam off to some religious sect where they worshipped who knows what on a mountain top and promised to drink pernicious brews in the face of certain calamities. But now I see for her a more normal life—white carpets, a wine rack, the generic family dog.

When I am especially tired and Bobby has kept me up until all hours, I think I've got it wrong. She has a house in Venice. She's a would-be actress, waitressing on the side, unashamed of her birthmark; she wears her hair pulled back, off her face, and has a strange, haunting look, like nothing anyone has ever seen. She wears her flaw proudly, like a flag.

At other times I picture something between these two ways of life. She's a social worker or a teacher of third grade. Two cats that her boyfriend is allergic to. Or a flight attendant, though who'd have her as a flight attendant with the birthmark? But there is something about Sam—probably the way she left me—that makes me see her disappearing into the clouds.

NINE

THERE IS A GHOST in Coal Mine Canyon and once my mother took me there. She said she had a special trip planned only for me, one that would take two days. Once again she dropped Sam off at Dottie's. It was the last time she would take me with her on one of her excursions into the desert, though of course I didn't know it at the time. I always felt—as I feel even now—that there would be one more outing, one more foray with my mother into the unknown.

This wasn't like our other excursions, when we seemed to amble along without a clear destination. This time my mother knew where she was going. It was dusk as we turned off into Hopiland, heading to the canyon where she promised that we'd see the ghost with the rising of the full moon. She had packed a picnic of store-bought fried chicken, potato chips, and pickles, and she drove to the rim of the canyon, where we ate our dinner. She poked me to stay awake.

For a long time we sat in the darkness. Then the full moon rose and the ghost's face appeared on the spectral rocks. At first she was elusive, but as the moon rose higher, she became clear. A woman, bent into herself and pensive, tears sliding down her cheeks, was etched in stone. She had flung herself off the canyon rim, where we sat, onto the rocks below. My mother told me to be quiet so that we could hear her crying. She had killed herself, my mother said, because of unrequited love or the death of her firstborn. No one knew for sure. But with the full moon, the light of her spirit shone through the rocks.

I must have fallen asleep near the canyon because it was morning when I woke in the car and we were on the road again. We crossed a desert that was drier and stranger than any I'd seen before—completely barren, with nothing growing. I drifted in and out of sleep, wondering where she was taking me. When I woke, it was late and we were in a deserted mining town. And there on a derelict strip of road was the house of junk.

It was shingled in broken glass, bottle caps, and street signs that read YIELD, BOMBING AREA: PREPARE TO EVACUATE, BLIND PEOPLE CROSSING, CURB YOUR DOG, and WOMEN ENTER AT YOUR OWN RISK. The house itself consisted of a shack and a trailer, joined by a patio. The patio was shaded with an old circus tent, supported by cacti and barber poles. It was illuminated with blinking lights and magic lanterns. Coconuts and Christmas ornaments dangled from the cacti. Silken birds perched in their branches and plastic pythons twisted around their trunks. A leaking overhead pipe formed a waterfall that tumbled over giant plastic fish and toads in a culvert where waterlilies grew. Streamers made from fliptops, eyelash curlers, hair rollers, and colored rubber bands were draped overhead. Old railroad lights flashed on and off.

"What is this place?" I asked, amazed. "How did you find it?"

She tossed her head back the way she did when she was pleased with herself. "Oh, I just came on it in my travels," as if she had seen the world and this was one of her many stops along the way.

A weathered man with bloodshot eyes and a beer belly hardly covered by a plaid workshirt emerged from the trailer. He grimaced in the light of the day as we walked toward him. Shading his eyes with one hand, he tried to determine who we were.

"Don't you remember me?" my mother said with a coy laugh. "I've been here before."

The man looked her up and down and smiled. "Yes." He nodded. "I do."

"This is my girl Ivy." She put a hand on my shoulder. "We're just passing through and wondered if you could put us up for the night."

He said it would be no problem. He seemed to like my mother, and he didn't mind me. He made us a very good dinner—huge plates of rice and beans and shredded beef—and afterward showed us to the guest room. The guest room consisted of a box spring and doublebed mattress on the flat roof of the trailer. Actually there were three such beds, in case he had several visitors. I looked up when he pointed to our room, startled, unable to believe that I would actually spend a night on his roof beneath the great expanse of western sky. Together, in the dark, my mother and I climbed up.

We pulled back the covers and curled up in cool sheets. There wasn't a cloud in the sky that night, and we lay together, heads resting on soft pillows under the stars. My mother held me to her. As I huddled in her arms, she pointed out the planets and constellations she knew. "That's Mars," she said with a laugh, pointing to a red planet. "I've been there. And there's the Archer; he looks like a teapot . . ."

She told me about a hunter who went off to shoot the big bear and about the scorpion that would bite your heel if you didn't walk swiftly in the dark. Of the winged horse that could carry you away if you catch his mane. And then she found Hercules, the Immortal Child. As I tried to follow her hand moving against the sky, she told me about a goddess who wanted to rule the world but found a baby left by the side of the road. The goddess picked him up and took pity on the adorable child. She nursed him, but Hercules clamped down so hard that she shrieked with pain and flung him off. Her milk splattered across the sky, making the Milky Way, but it was too late. Hercules was immortal.

Everything has a story, my mother told me that night. But how she came to know the stories of the ghosts who lived in canyons or the creatures of the sky I'll never know. Maybe someone had told them to her one night when she was a girl.

She seemed content as she talked, happy to be with me. Her palms were rough against my face, cracked as an alkali flat, but she smelled fresh, as if a storm had just passed through. She held me so tight that I could scarcely breathe. I thought that I could just stay there forever under the stars. If she asks me now, I thought to myself, whether I want to keep going, I'll say yes. I knew that night I'd have no trouble saying yes.

TEN

THE DAY IN APRIL when Matthew called, it was snowing—a last, sad burst of winter. I was sitting at the window, working on a tedious piece—a medieval collar—from the Brooklyn Museum. Outside, large, unseasonable clumps of snow fell, covering the forsythia already blooming beneath my window, the sprouting daffodils and tulips that the woman across the way had planted the summer before her husband left. I watched her go downstairs, trying to brush the snow away.

The collar was slow, exacting work and I was having trouble with it. Also, I wanted to be working on a collage that had preoccupied me of late. It was to be a dark image, a desert at night, with an open road, an illegible street sign, Day-Glo stars, and, of course, buried in the background, the face. I had merely sketched it out and I wanted to begin applying color, but Bobby had had a bad night.

He seemed to be having a bout of stomach flu; he'd been vomiting and had hardly slept, which meant that I had hardly slept. Nor had I been able to paint. My eyes were sore and I wanted to lie down and nap when he did, but I needed to get some work done. I was contemplating taking him to the pediatrician, but a simple visit for a doctor to say he needed to rest and take fluids would cost me fifty dollars, and besides I didn't think I should take him out in the snow. I figured, if I was lucky, I had two hours before he woke.

When the phone rang, I grabbed it before it could wake Bobby. "Hello," I said.

"Ivy," a voice said, "it's me."

The phone trembled in my hand. "What is it?" I said. "What do you want?"

The last I had seen or talked with Matthew was two days after Bobby was born. I had asked him to go to the Office of Birth Records and sign the affidavit, legalizing his paternity. Matthew had balked, so I told him not to call me again unless he changed his mind. The day I was going home, I signed my son's birth certificate by myself, sobbing —the space for the father's name left blank. I had grabbed a name out of the air—Robert Ethan Slovak. The nurse stood there, holding out her hand, waiting. She patted me on the shoulder. "You'll feel better," she said, "when your husband gets here." Instead, Dottie and my father, who'd come from their retirement home in Arizona, took me home from the hospital. Now I wanted to put the receiver down, but I was so tired. It was as if I didn't have the strength. "What do you want?"

"I want to see you," he said.

"There's no reason to see me unless you want to do things differently."

"I've been thinking"—he spoke hesitantly—"I've been thinking maybe I do." Then he added, "I miss you. It's not the same."

"It hasn't been the same for a long time." I spoke softly. "I miss you, too, but I don't want to hear from you."

"Look, could I see you? I haven't seen you since Bobby was born. Could I come over?"

I sighed. "If you have something different to say or if you'd like to sign the papers for Bobby, you can come over."

"You drive a hard bargain. You didn't used to be this way."

I thought about that. It was true. I had been easier once, but then my life had been easier. "I've learned to make hard choices."

"Are you all right? Are you making out?"

"I'm all right," I said, wondering how to answer his questions. "I'm very tired; I didn't think I could be this tired."

"Maybe I could help you out a little?" he said. "Could I come by? Just once?"

"Was it you?" I asked. "Did you call me at night and hang up?"

There was silence on the other end. "I called once or twice," he said, "but I was afraid to say anything."

When we got off the phone, it was still snowing. The last time it snowed was a couple of months ago, the night Bobby was born. Babies come in snowstorms, I'd heard. It has to do with changes in pressure, the tug on the earth. That afternoon I'd gone to the park, lain on my back, made snow angels. But I hadn't felt right. My muscles ached; my limbs were inexplicably heavy.

The night he was born was the third night in a row that I hadn't slept. When I told that to Dottie, phoning from Tucson, her voice cracked and gravelly across the miles, she said, "The baby's coming now." It wasn't possible, I told her. "It's coming," she said. It was nearly a month early, but my water broke that night, and I wasn't prepared. I sat at the edge of the bed and wept bitter tears. I had nothing for this eventuality—no crib, no bottles, no clothes. I'd been planning to do everything in the last few weeks.

As I felt my labor worsening, I rose and went to the window. I would have to leave soon. I breathed deeply. It was the middle of the night. Pitch black. A cold city landscape outside with drifts piled high. With great effort I turned and went to the mirror and ran a brush through my curls. My father hadn't called me Lucky Red for nothing, I thought, as pain clasped me again.

I took out a small suitcase, the same little green suitcase my father used to have me pack during those endless escapes in my itinerant youth. It was the suitcase I clutched that carried my life's possessions, such as they were, when we left town for a day, a week, or forever. Though it had been a long time since I'd gone anywhere, I was surprised at the skill that returned as I packed quickly in the middle of the night.

I did it methodically, running a checklist through my mind. Toothbrush, underwear, nightgown, address book. Comb, brush, change of clothes. A Russian novel I'd planned to read—and now seemed as good a time as any. Jasmine perfume, soft slippers. I could be going to a slumber party or to a weekend tryst, a small business trip, but it was none of the above.

When I was ready, I gave a deep sigh. I should call somebody. My father. Patricia or an upstairs neighbor. Of course I should call my birth coach, who'd seen me through two Lamaze classes. What about Matthew? I vowed I would not call him. Let the others sleep, I told myself. They'll need their rest. I picked up the suitcase and headed outside, gripping the railing of the building. Beside me the garbage was overturned, picked through. A shirt nobody wanted, last year's magazines, scattered scraps of food.

It was four A.M. and freezing cold as I made my way down the street. I had never been out this late alone and was amazed at how quiet the city was. There was hardly a sound on the deserted streets. Pausing against a streetlamp, I looked up at the darkened windows where for the most part people lived alone in one or two small rooms. Gazing upward, I saw a low layer of clouds, those yellowish-white clouds which bode snow. City lights reflected off them. There were no stars. Somewhere in the distance I heard the sound of shattering glass. A car alarm went off. I hailed a cab, and the driver, on his way home perhaps, pulled over. He stared at the suitcase in my hand. "I'm not going to the airport, lady," he said.

"Neither am I," I replied, getting in.

I told him where to go. He looked at me oddly, shaking his head. Then he drove slowly through the snowbound streets. The city was all shades and contrasts, a study in black and white, like a Stieglitz. Matthew would have appreciated this observation. I'd never seen snow as a child. I'd never known the way it comes fluttering down. Whenever it snows, I tilt my head back and let the flakes light on my tongue. Once when I was falling in love with Matthew, he told me that in winter he put on his skates to go to the house of his friends. This had seemed part of a fairy tale to me, for in my youth I had walked only the burning roads, and friends were few and far between, scattered in dusty trailer parks.

The driver grumbled as he drove. "Snow," he

said. "Do you know what it does to my business? Do you know how much money I lose?"

A plow was ahead of us, blade down. The sound of the scraping was muted. Snow fell in all directions. The driver once again complained. "It's all right," I said. "I'm not in a hurry. In fact, I'd prefer it if you'd take your time." I should have borrowed cross-country skis and sailed to this appointment. I could have dallied in the park. Made a snow fortress. Packed myself in. Or lain on my back again and made snow angels. I felt invincible, a blessed being, as if no harm could come my way.

Another pain gripped me. As the driver cursed the icy road that made his journey treacherous and slow, I clutched my sides, trying to breathe and wondering what kind of mother I would be. The kind who takes the kid on summer vacations, packing him into a van and off to the national parks. Who takes dozens of snapshots on rope swings, wading in mountain streams, then pastes them into leather-bound albums with gold initials on the outside. Labeling pages on the kitchen table late at night. Jersey Shore, summer. Aged four. Aged eight.

But perhaps I'd be a different kind of mother. One who drags the kid off to bars or brings in the endless parade of lovers, all called Uncle This or Uncle That, filling the house with strange men so that my child would wake in the morning to someone he'd never seen before, someone sipping coffee at the Formica table, hiding behind newspapers. Never knowing if a man would take him out to play ball or shoo him away.

At last the cab came to a halt, but I wanted the driver to keep going. To drive through the park again. I had time, I thought. Take me just once more around. Or better yet, drop me off in the middle of a snowy field. I'll have my baby there in the open, in the blistering cold. Then I'll bring him quickly to my warm breast.

Instead, I grabbed my bag and handed the driver a bill. "I can't change a twenty," he said, handing it back to me.

One more sharp pain went through me. "Keep the change," I said, shoving it back to him through the bulletproof drawer. Stepping out, I took a deep breath. It would be a long time before I'd stand outside by myself again in the middle of the night like this. Breathing in deeply the night air, I gazed at the yellow sky. It was almost morning. I picked up my suitcase and walked toward the emergency room doors.

The buzzer rang and I opened the door hesitantly, regretting it even as I did so. Matthew stood in the doorway, dressed in jeans and a green leather jacket, a flannel shirt. I stepped out of the way, motioning for him to come in, not sure whether I wanted him to or not. He stooped, kissing me on the cheek, then on the lips, and walked in. "You look well, Ivy," he said. "You look very good."

"All things considered," I replied.

"No, you just look good."

"Not sleeping agrees with me," I said.

He shrugged. "I'm just happy to see you; that's all."

On our way to the restaurant we hardly spoke. We stuck to innocuous topics, walking gingerly around the edges of whatever we had to say. "They're talking about putting a new water main down my street," I said at one point. His hand rested on my shoulder as I walked with Bobby in his Snugli. It was one of the first times I'd gone out to dinner since Bobby was born. I'd been to Patricia's, I'd been out once or twice with friends for pizza and with Dottie and my father when they came just after Bobby was born. Just before Matthew arrived, I'd struggled to get into a pair of pre-Bobby jeans but settled for a loose-fitting skirt. I put on red lipstick.

We went to a neighborhood Chinese restaurant where we instinctively selected our old favorites— General's Chicken, Sesame Noodles, Shrimp with Snowpeas.

"So," I said once we'd ordered and a glass of free wine arrived, "how's your work going?"

"Oh." Matthew cocked his head the way he did when he couldn't admit to being disappointed.

"I'm getting a lot of foreign assignments for magazines."

"And your own work?"

Now he cocked his head the other way. "It doesn't exactly pay the bills."

I nodded and we grew silent, neither of us wanting to mention the bills. Money was on my mind; I needed some if I was going to hire a baby sitter and return to work full time. Normally I would have asked him outright, but we were being tentative with each other, like distant relatives brought together over some delicate legal matter, which in a sense we were. I draped a napkin over Bobby's head and tried, as I ate with my chopsticks, not to drop steamed rice on him. When Bobby woke and I had to nurse him, Matthew fed me with a fork.

He ran his hand through his silvery curls. He looked older than I remembered, though it hadn't been that long since I'd seen him. "Ivy." He put the fork down. Like my mother, Matthew always said my name before he said anything else to me. And he pronounced it "IV," the way she did, as if I were a form of life support. "My mother phoned the other day" he began. "Her voice was shaky. Her speech was slurred. 'Matthew,' she said, 'whatever happened to that nice girl, Ivy. I always liked her.' I could hear airplanes flying in the background. She lives right near this airport and planes are always taking off and landing. Anyway, she said, 'Ivy was good for you. She was the best of the lot, because you were nicer to me when you were with her. You remembered my birthday, holidays . . .' "

"I just kept a calendar by the phone," I said.

"Well, my mother thinks I made a big mistake."

"Does she know about Bobby?"

He looked grim. "She knows. But she has trouble remembering. That's what booze does for you." He took a deep breath, then reached across the table for my hand. "When I was a little boy," he said as if I'd never heard of it before, "my parents stayed in bed all day long on the weekends. They drank and screwed and stayed in bed. No one played with me. I learned to cook, take care of my things, play alone. My room just had a bed and a desk. Like a monk's cell. No pictures on the walls. No toys. A few books. I had a fish tank with no fish in it. I was the only sober person around. I took care of myself. I had to learn to do that at an early age. I'm not very good at taking care of others."

I nodded. "I hear it's an acquired skill."

"Maybe, but I'm not sure I've acquired it."

"Matthew." I squeezed his hand, then pulled mine away. "You aren't telling me anything I don't already know. Do you want me to feel sorry for you?"

"I just wanted you to know that I think my

mother was right. I think I did make a big mistake." And he leaned over and kissed me.

Then we went home. When it was time for me to tuck Bobby in, Matthew stayed. "I should get going," he said, but he didn't leave. He stayed as I cuddled Bobby, nursing him and singing as I put him to sleep. Matthew went with me into the room where Bobby slept and watched as I put him down. Together we stared at the sleeping child. When Bobby slept, he breathed heavily, his chest heaving as if he were already a man. Little beads of sweat broke out along the rim of his dark hair, and Matthew and I stood watching our son.

"Is he all right?" Matthew asked, listening to his breathing and touching his son's sweat.

"He's like you," I told him, thinking how much they did resemble one another. "You sleep just like this."

I pulled the covers up to Bobby's chin, though Bobby—a warm-blooded creature like his father—would kick them off in the night. We stood silently, watching the child. Soon I felt Matthew's fingers wrapping themselves around mine, as we remained side by side, looking down at the baby. I'm not sure how long we stood there before he said, "I love you, Ivy. You know I do." And of course I did.

He turned me to him and kissed me. His tongue reached deep into my mouth; his hands gripped my back, holding me firm. He was hard, throbbing against my thigh, and he held me to him for a long time, which I did not mind because I didn't know what I wanted to happen next. My heart beat quickly, but not from desire. Rather, it pounded the way it did when someone jumped out of a dark corner and frightened me.

"Is this the right thing?" I asked, pulling away.

He stood back so that he could see my face. "I want you," he said, "But more than that, I'd like to try again. I'd like to spend time with you"—he paused—"and with Bobby." He looked down sheepishly, as if he'd just confessed to a pointless lie.

"Are you sure?"

"I'm not completely sure. I'm never sure of anything. I can't make any promises."

I smiled, putting my fingers to his lips. "You never could."

I wanted to ask him to leave, but I was surprised by a wave that rushed over me, as warm and comforting as when my milk let down, yet with an urgency I hadn't felt in a long time. Not since I was a girl, I thought, sneaking out of the house to meet boys I scarcely knew in places where I wasn't supposed to be. There was something dangerous, something slightly naughty about what I felt. Now he pulled me close so that my head rested against his shoulder. Gently he touched my breasts, which were heavy and sore.

We made love slowly as if it were our first time,

and indeed it was the first time since I'd gone to his studio when I was four months pregnant. My body seemed huge, my breasts full, and the slowness suited my mood and my physical state. It wasn't exactly desire I felt, for motherhood had sapped and supplemented much of that, but it was a kind of comfort I had not experienced in a long while. As he sucked on my breasts, the milk flowed and he told me it was sweet as coconut juice. This made him more tender with me. He entered me gently, careful not to cause any pain, and he stayed inside for a long time.

Afterward we lay in each other's arms until Bobby cried. "Don't get up," Matthew said. "I'll go. You rest." Matthew took Bobby onto his shoulder. I lay still, watching them. Matthew warmed a bottle on the stove as he clumsily cradled Bobby. He would grow accustomed to this. In a few months he would see. Life could go on. He would be a good father. It would come naturally.

He gave the baby the bottle, but Bobby fussed, spitting out the milk. "It's all right," I said. "He wants me." So Matthew brought him to the bed. Another warm wave rushed over me as milk filled my breasts. The sensation that had once caused me so much pain now came with intense pleasure. Matthew put Bobby next to me and turned out the light. We lay there, the three of us together. Bobby's damp hair smelled like a puppy's. A kind of peace came over me as I felt hands at my breasts, mouths sucking, unsure if it were my lover or my son or both, who touched, who suckled, and, somehow nursing both of them, I drifted in and out of sleep.

After a while, I eased my way out of bed, leaving Matthew and Bobby on separate pillows. They lay like bookends, face to face, mirror images of each other, though I didn't want to admit it. I went to the mirror and saw my body in the moonlight. It was a strange body, foreign to me, thicker than I remembered it. My breasts looked pendulous, like the hanging teats of stray dogs I used to throw stones at as a child. But now I could see the beginning of a waistline, the shape of my hips. I gazed at this body again as if it belonged to me once more, as if it were being given back, slowly, a little at a time.

Putting on a robe, I went to the window and sat down at my work table with the collage—the desert at night, the Day-Glo stars. Picking up a pencil, I started to draw. But I felt as if someone were watching me, so I looked up. She was standing in her window, trim body pressed against the sill, her hair down to her shoulders. Perhaps her husband was coming to get the kids and she was watching for him. Perhaps a lover was coming to visit and she didn't want him to ring the bell. Then I feared that she was desperate, planning to jump. I waved a finger at her. "No, no," I whispered. Now she looked my way. I put the pencil down and for the first time our eyes met. I'm not sure how long we stared at each other in this way.

It was Matthew who had brought me east. I probably would never have come if he hadn't gotten the teaching job at a respectable center for photography and said he was moving to New York. He had just done his Hall of Fame project. He'd driven around the American West for months (sometimes I went along), taking pictures of all the Halls of Fame in America—the Greyhound Hall of Fame, the Corn Growers, football, cowboys, stuntmen, American plastics industry, the Furriers of North America.

The pictures varied, but usually they included the front of the building and a major organizer or representative. For example, for the Greyhound Hall of Fame he had a famous breeder and a very old greyhound—a scrawny thing with splotchy fur that had once had a great racing career. The Furriers stood in elegant fur coats, caressing small, nervous beasts. He was offered the teaching job right after that show, though not much has happened in his career since that.

We had been together for a little more than a year in Los Angeles. Before I met Matthew, I had been with many men. My father and Dottie and I moved back to California when I was sixteen, and while they thought I was going out with friends, I was sneaking in and out of the arms of strange men on hilltops, in bungalows, on the beaches of Los Angeles. I was the perfect student. I got straight A's. And at night I slipped out and smoked dope with the Mexican gangs on the Venice Boardwalk. It was a kind of fix, something I had to have, though I was always attached to the ones who drifted away.

Then I met Matthew. I wasn't drawn to him at first. We met at the art college where Dottie had sent me years before and where I returned to take courses from time to time. He was the second person—after Dottie—who'd taken an interest in my art. He commented on what he saw, telling me what he would change. How he thought I could improve a design. He made his suggestions simply, never pressing a point. Yet his instincts about my work were always right. We saw each other for weeks, often spending our time together at galleries and museums, before we went to bed.

When we began seeing each other, he was punctual, always on time. Within five minutes of when he said he'd be there, the buzzer would ring. If he was late, he'd phone with an explanation. This was important to me, because I never wondered in the early months whether he would show, whether he planned to leave.

But gradually, his behavior began to change and this tied me to him more and more. He arrived a little late. Ten minutes, half an hour. Then he'd show up on time. Then forty-five minutes late.

There were always good reasons—a car breaking down, a client's last-minute request. But I found myself at home, waiting to hear from him, afraid that he would not arrive. Fear began to rule my feelings. First I had wanted Matthew because I knew he would not leave me. Then I wanted him because I knew he would.

When Matthew decided to move east, I told him I wanted to go with him. Nothing was holding me in California. My father and Dottie had already moved outside of Tucson so that she could be close to her son, Jamie, a management consultant, and her grandchildren, twin boys. "Do you want me to come?" I asked Matthew. At times he said yes and at other times no. He was going, no matter what. In the end he told me, "It's a big decision. I want you to do what's right for you."

We made the move smoothly enough. We put whatever mattered—a few duffels, cameras, tools, art supplies—into our two cars and caravaned across the United States. I liked traveling this way, actually; one of us was always just ahead of the other or just behind. We drove hundreds of miles a day, waving at each other. We used elaborate hand signals when we needed to stop for gas, to go to the bathroom, to rest. We signed to each other as I left behind everything I had known.

There is a moment when you drive through a rocky pass on the interstate and find yourself facing nothing but a thousand miles or more of flat, yellow prairie, with the mountains now at your back. We reached that point—and the West was behind me. It was as if I had grown up while we traversed that divide, passed through a dimension of time, and I was surprised by how ready I was to give up all that had been my life. Still, the moment we arrived in New York, I wanted to leave. I felt certain it would never be a place I'd call home—not that I've ever had such a place.

Matthew has a spot he calls home. It is a red brick house on a tree-lined street on the outskirts of Minneapolis. It is here he claims that hell was played out in the form of an alcoholic, abusive father and a passive, ineffectual, but also alcoholic, mother. But Matthew has a fierce attachment to this house and this suburb, and on our drive east we went some five hundred miles out of our way to see his home.

We drove through Matthew's neighborhood, which looked as if it had become an extension of the inner city. The river that flowed through the back of the town was littered with debris. A garbage dump had appeared along its banks. The school Matthew had gone to was scarred with graffiti. Matthew was bewildered by what he saw.

The house itself was run-down, the shutters in need of painting and repair. Broken toys and pieces of a lawn mower were scattered across the lawn. A mangy dog lay on the porch, which was missing some boards. Matthew stood in front of the house for a long time, looking toward the river, the river on which he had skated as a boy with his friends. He drew his strength, he told me as we leaned against a tree in front of the house, from here.

I have no such place filled with the images of my youth. No large tree with the boards of an old tree house in its branches, no broken-down school covered with racial slurs, no memory of a river to make it all seem real. There is no single place to which I can attach the importance of all that has been. Once in a while I used to stop near the bungalow in Venice where we lived for a few years, or drive past the Valley of Fire trailer park when we were in Vegas, but I always felt as if someone else had lived there.

My childhood was lived among rocks and insects, and under the canopy of stars. The strange, twisted cacti, the lizards who bite and will never let go unless you chop off their heads. I used to flick scorpions away with my fingers. There was a small bug I collected and kept in jars. The one everyone thought was poisonous, but it wasn't. Child of the Earth, it was called. It was a cricket, but it had the bald, smiling face of a child. When you stepped on it, it screamed. That was home to me.

ELEVEN

MUCH OF WHITE SANDS is a missile range that the army uses for target practice. Trinity Site, where the first nuclear bomb was detonated in 1945, is here. So is a range of mountains called Jornada del Muerto, the Hills of the Dead. When you drive west from Alamagordo, you can hear missiles whizzing across the highway. But the day when we snuck in, it was quiet.

It was the summer my father locked the door of the trailer, saying he had to find work, but probably because he had to leave town. We spent much of the summer driving through the Southwest— into Arizona, across the Navajo and Apache and Zuñi reserves. My father was very good at fixing things—refrigerators, toasters, old TVs—and the Indians had plenty of those appliances, which they had picked up cheap from gringo traders and which often didn't work. We'd eat a meal of fry bread and beans while he fixed a woman's washing machine. While my mother sat fanning herself in doorways, Sam and I played with the Indian children, who lived on dirt floors and had runny noses.

My father put a sign on the side of the Dodge sedan he drove, a car that probably had a hundred thousand miles on it when it finally gave out. I CAN FIX ANYTHING, it said. When we got into the car to leave Vegas, my mother had sneered at the sign. "You can fix anything except what matters," she said.

It was stifling in the car. Sam and I tried counting red cars or blue cars, but lost ourselves past ten. Our mother sat in the passenger seat, which was not her preferred locale (since she was somewhat addicted to driving), smoking cigarettes in silence, letting the ashes blow into the back seat, where Sam and I batted at the dying embers. One landed on Sam's arm and left a small black burn. She rubbed it for miles.

A scorching breeze blew and we found respite for only a week when we moved into an abandoned Dairy Queen outside Rincon. Even in the heat of the summer, the freezer of the Dairy Queen where Sam and I slept was nice and cool. The freezer had had its door ripped off, and we could enter that soothing darkness whenever we wanted to rest. At night Sam and I cuddled in a sleeping bag inside the freezer which smelled faintly of old chocolate and peppermint.

Sam and I loved the red and white of the Dairy Queen, the soda machines. We spent our afternoons pretending I was the soda jerk, since I was the older, and Sam was the customer. We asked our mother to be the customer, but she refused. Instead, she sat in a chair that had been left behind under a juniper tree, watching cars speed up and down the highway. She kept her hand over her eyes like a sea captain, searching for land as the cars disappeared, dwindling to nothing. The desert even looked like an ocean, a rippling sea. Once a man with his kids in the car, seeing us there, stopped. He was hot and desperate as he tried to order ice cream cones. "What flavor, mister?" my mother said as she laughed and laughed.

Sam ordered the usual things from me, like strawberry floats and black cows, which I pretended to make with complicated gestures. Sometimes I let Sam concoct things. We made a huge banana split in a boat with whipped cream heaped high like a castle, a rosy cherry bleeding from the top. This we brought out to our mother as she sat beneath the juniper tree. She stared into our empty hands. "There's nothing there," she said.

"Yes," Sam said. "It's a banana split with the works."

Our mother sighed and took a bite with an imaginary spoon. "Oh, it's very good." She took another bite. "And cool." She licked her fingers. She seemed to enjoy the taste. Then she gathered us into her arms. "My precious girls," she said. "My precious little girls."

White Sands wasn't far from the Dairy Queen, and one day my father took us there. He'd been out most of the day before, driving around looking for work. "Guess what?" he said when he came home. "I found something you girls are going to like." There was a place along the highway where the sand had drifted. We pulled the car off the road, climbed over the fence, and raced across the ridges of what had once been the bottom of a gypsum sea.

Before us everything was bleached white with no trees, no animals, no signs of life. Nothing but this soft, pristine mattress of sand, where we leaped, tumbling head over heels, but never hurting ourselves. I have pictures from this day. We are sun-drenched, flaming children against the shimmering white sands. Our faces are full of laughter, without a hint of what lies ahead.

My mother is not in these photographs—though my father is, as he rolls down the dunes, his hair also blazing in the sun, sand flung around his face —so she must have taken them. The only trace of her is a shoulder turned away as she twists down an embankment.

The one picture I have of my mother's face is on a passport. My father burned the rest. There are two interesting things about the passport—other than the fact that it exists. The first is that my mother has lied about the date of her birth, making herself younger than her age, which wasn't that old to start with. The other is that it is a virgin passport, unblemished, devoid of marks. The clean, blank pages of an uneventful life.

Not many people can take a passport photo the way my mother did. She stares into the camera, dead on. Her dark eyes are set straight ahead as if she were daring the person to take her picture. An Ava Gardner lookalike, Dottie once said. A woman who could easily be mistaken for someone else. Sometimes I stare at the passport photo and try to decipher the enigma behind the eyes. I try to understand what moved her to get a passport anyway, when she was living in San Bernardino in a trailer with a small child, another on the way. Whatever could have prompted her to do such a thing, since she must have known she wouldn't be going anywhere. Not for a while.

In the photograph my mother still had long black hair. It was thick and silken, like the kind Rapunzel's knight used to climb the tower. At night she would sit in front of a small, misty mirror in her room of the trailer and brush her hair for hours. When she brushed it, she got a dreamy look, as if she were listening to something far away.

If I asked, she would let me brush it. "You can

do it tonight, Ivy. I'm so tired." And she'd hand me her brush with the soft bristles. I ran the brush through over and over again and she closed her eyes as if she were starting to sleep. When I put down the brush and rubbed her scalp with my fingers, she'd tilt her head back and moan. I'd rub her cheeks, her jaw. My mother rarely liked me to crawl into bed with her or curl up in her lap, but she'd let me brush her hair and rub her scalp for a long time.

Once, in Vegas, Sam and I took all her barrettes and fine brushes and spent the afternoon fixing our hair the way she did. Often Sam and I did things we weren't supposed to do, like walk into the desert late in the day, thrusting sticks down the rattlesnake holes. But usually when we were caught and punished, it was for something insig-nificant—watching television after school or dress-ing up in our mother's clothes. Or using her combs and barrettes.

My mother got angry about little things—if we left the light on or didn't close a cupboard door. But what really enraged her was if we touched the objects that adorned her hair. For some reason Sam always got caught, and I seldom did. Sam would stand at the sink, tears streaming down her face, while our mother scolded her for something we both knew I'd done.

This time she scolded Sam for the barrettes and combs I'd put in her hair. Sam cried but did not tell. I expected her to just blurt it out. Maybe she thought I'd confess. But Sam never told. She could fight for any resistance movement, I'm sure. Loyal, that's how I'd describe my sister.

As my mother stood over Sam, trying to make her confess, she held a spatula in her hand, not that she ever struck us—she wasn't that kind of mother—and stared a terrifying stare, not unlike the one in her passport photo. She said something like "You better tell me why you did this, young lady. You better have a good explanation."

Suddenly, in the middle of her outburst, my mother sighed, as if she'd lost interest in what she thought Sam had done. As if none of it really mattered. And maybe it didn't. She lay down and asked us to bring her a wet washcloth. "This heat is killing me," she said. We brought her a cloth, which she pressed to her forehead. After a while, she pulled back the curtain and gazed out into the desert. "Just look at that ocean, those city lights, the Avenue of the Stars." Sam and I gazed with her down the empty streets of a dusty gambling town, watching the glamorous people my mother saw parading by.

One night shortly after we'd returned to Vegas from our summer on the road, I was brushing my mother's hair and she made me stop. She took the brush away and stared into the mirror as if she saw something that made her afraid. She ran her fingers over her eyes, her mouth. "I'm getting old," she said. I took back the brush and stroked her hair longer than before. I took thick strands, pinning them high on her head.

A few days later she came home with her hair cut off. It was up to her ears and there was nothing for me to brush or braid. She never again asked me to rub her head or touch her. Later it occurred to me that she had sold the hair—hair like hers still went for about $200 a braid, even then. It was the money that helped finance her escape.

Shortly after she cut her hair, I was invited to a party, and my mother said I should have a new dress. She seemed suddenly to have cash to burn, and told me I could have whatever kind of dress I wanted. I said I wanted a blue dress with flowers, so she took the day off from the At First Sight marriage chapel, where she was working at the time, and we went to a store in the shopping center. I was to take my time, she said, and try on all the dresses until I found just what I wanted.

She was very patient with me that day. I tried on dozens of dresses we had no intention of buying—green chiffon with a satin bodice, a flowing red that made me look like a dance hall girl, a black cocktail dress for a woman three times my age, a pink ruffled thing for the young and innocent. I tried them all on until I found the one I liked—blue with a white crinoline and blue flowers.

The saleswoman carefully folded the dress into a box, which we carried to a place called Buffalo's, where we had ice cream. I ordered a double banana split with whipped cream, the kind Sam and I had pretended to make when we lived in the Dairy Queen. It came in a boat-shaped dish, looking as if it could sail away. I expected my mother to light a cigarette and talk in choppy, nervous sentences. Usually she asked question after question, never waiting for my answers, which floated in the air. Her attention span always seemed to be about the length of a cigarette, whether she was smoking or not.

But this afternoon she leaned on her elbows, looking at me intently. There was something sad about her, something wistful, and it seemed to me that, perhaps for the first time, my mother wanted to listen. That she heard what I was trying to say. She sipped her Coke and now and then put her finger in my whipped cream, slowly licking it off.

She said, "You're going to be the prettiest girl at the party." She said it again and again, as if she were giving me instructions that I was to commit to memory. "You are going to be the prettiest and all the boys will want to dance with you." But by the day of the party my mother was gone, and the dress hung in my closet, unworn, for years.

TWELVE

MATTHEW didn't want to attend the Lamaze class reunion. He said what's the point. He hadn't attended any of the classes, not that I had attended that many myself. It would look odd, he said. And Jake, my longtime friend and birth coach, whom the class had assumed to be my husband, was out of town. When they phoned me for the reunion, I was surprised, since I'd made it through only two classes. A woman named Irene, whom I had no recollection of, phoned to say that she and her husband were hosting the reunion at their place on Central Park West and wondered if Jake and I would attend.

"You disappeared," Irene said on the phone.

I was taken aback. "I beg your pardon?"

"You were there, then you were gone."

"My baby came early."

"Nobody talked about you," she said in a

whisper. "It was as if you'd died. Mrs. Volkan wouldn't mention it."

"I had a caesarean."

"Oh," Irene said, pity in her voice, "that's why."

The reunion was being held on a Saturday afternoon, and I didn't want to go alone, but Matthew didn't think it would be appropriate for him to accompany me. "I mean, who would they think I was? Wouldn't it look strange?"

"We could make up a story. How you were off somewhere and I didn't want to explain . . ."

"Ivy"—Matthew squeezed my arm—"it's just not my kind of thing."

"It's not my kind of thing either," I said.

On Saturday I arrived late at the building on Central Park West. The austere, pasty-faced doorman announced me as I entered the marble entranceway, Bobby in his stroller. He carted the stroller up the two steps, making me wish for the first time that I lived in a doorman building. The elevator, which moved effortlessly between floors, was lined with gilded overhead mirrors and recessed track lighting. Muzak filled its hollow space. Bobby cooed to the sounds of Burt Bacharach's "Raindrops Keep Falling on My Head." I could live in this elevator, that's how nice it was. Bobby was soothed by the music, bobbing his head now to an old Beatles song, and I stared at my face in the mirror in the flattering light, thinking that I looked well; my eyes seemed to sparkle, my skin glowed.

The door was open, so I walked in. Through the entranceway my feet glided as if on a cloud of creamy white carpet with pink trim as I made my silent approach across a long stretch of thin blue industrial into the living room, with its wall-to-wall yellow shag, dense and flowing as prairie grass.

Irene's husband, Hal, was in the carpet business, I recalled as she greeted me on the yellow shag, holding up Alissa, a perplexed blond child with peach-fuzz hair. Alissa, who was a few weeks younger than Bobby, wore a kind of elastic headband with a pink bow that was causing a ridge to rise on her pale skull. She kept reaching up, as if trying to pluck it away, and Irene kept pushing her hand down. "Oh, we're so glad you could make it. Oh, isn't he cute." She tickled Bobby under the chin. "He looks just like his father, doesn't he?"

"His father?" I asked dumbly, wondering how she knew.

"Yes, Jake, your husband. He couldn't make it?"

"Oh, Jake. No, he's away on business. He has a lot of accounts in the Orient." I stared at Bobby, trying to determine if he looked like Jake.

"Oh?" Irene looked perplexed. "I thought he was a sociologist."

· 126 ·

I mumbled something about his being a sociologist who advised foreign governments, then followed her into the den, with its dark green dirt-resilient carpeting, on which a dozen new additions to the human race lay. Standing in their midst was a gigantic wooden rocking horse, looking life-sized, its runners grazing perilously close to the tiny, fragile skulls. "Oh, aren't they cute!" I exclaimed as six couples who had made it to the reunion, all evenly matched, beamed at me. I made number thirteen as I entered the room.

The children lay in various states of confusion, this being the first party for those who had not been publicly circumcised, immersed in water, or shown off to an endless parade of doting relatives. What was it like to be so small and see all those lights going off in your face? To see this giant horse hovering and all these giants ogling you, tickling, pinching?

Bobby seemed to resist such displays. At first he grew passive and limp in my arms, the way some animals do under attack, when they surrender by playing dead. He had no interest in the limelight, even the flash of his reluctant father's camera. He was a more self-contained type, happy to gaze into space for hours, to watch a sudden flight of birds. Once I saw his eyes moving against the sky, and I put my head where his lay and saw what my son saw—the clouds rolling by. This entertained him for a good hour, impressing me with his attention span.

Now he took one look at the huge rocking horse, the half-dozen "rug rats," as my father referred to babies, helpless on the floor, the parents beaming all around—and screamed. "There, there." I patted him. "It's all right." The parents stared, sad smiles on their faces as I tried to calm my tormented child, the only one who had made a scene thus far. Without their name tags on, the parents were all just faces. I couldn't tell Donna and Dick from Marian and Martin. Who were the microbiologists? The advertising executives with their own firm? Their vacant stares made me think I had been brought in to entertain them— the party act.

The first time I had laid eyes on any of these strangers—people with whom I would never have been in the same room had we not somehow booked passage on the same cruise—was for my first and next-to-last Lamaze class. Jake had accompanied me as I walked into the room holding his hand, staring at nine couples, all of whom looked as if they sold municipal bonds. (Several did.) Well-pressed yuppies, blissful in their prenatal state, had gaped at me that night as I ran sobbing out the door. "Hormones," Jake had explained as he rushed out. He caught up with me on the sidewalk. "Tell me your doctor's name, your due date, what hospital." "Glickoff, Valentine's Day, Lenox Hill," I told him. Then he took me back to the only class in my life from which I could consider myself a dropout.

Irene took me by the arm. "This is Ivy," she said. "You remember her, the jeweler. Now she's Bobby's mother." They all smiled as they tried to remember me, relaxed now that Bobby had stopped crying. "The baby came early," Irene offered as an explanation. Everyone was introduced, the children first. I met Alexis, Nathaniel, Angelica, Whisper. (I had to ask twice. Whisper? Her parents grinned, proud of their choice. "No one else will have that name," her father said.)

Next, the parents were introduced again, but they had become, for all practical purposes, Alexis's mother, Angelica's father. We were no longer adults with a past, not real people anymore, but the products of our own progeny. Everything that had happened before in our lives was suddenly obliterated—our jobs, our quirks of personality, our yearnings and passions, even our names. None of that had any significance in this new world to which I was suddenly being initiated, the world in which I would be Bobby's mother for the years to come. In Lamaze class I had felt we nine couples were like those in a war, thrown together in the trenches for no reason other than our common fate.

We looked at one another solemnly, strangers linked by fate. The reason for being in the same room had come into the light. Irene and Hal had set up a small buffet of cheese, crackers, cookies, apple juice, milk in paper cups—children's food, though our children were much too young to enjoy it—and the parents milled about.

"I remember. You did leave after a couple of classes," an attractive blond woman said, an actress who lived in Connecticut.

"Bobby came early. I had a caesarean."

A hush came over the room. "Premature?" someone spoke hesitantly.

"Oh, no, just early," I said cheerfully.

But again I got the troubled stares, for I had said the word that had been like an expletive or insult to our teacher, Mrs. Volkan, the Austrian woman who never let it be uttered in her classes. It was strictly *verboten*. It had the same impact as phrases like "terminal illness" and "all-out nuclear war." It was the word to describe those who, despite themselves, had somehow failed.

Now we began to talk openly about our plights. Three of the women had had C-sections. Out of the four who'd had natural childbirth, two said that they had forgotten their breathing once the real pain of transition set in. "You know what Michele did," said the man married to the actress. "She bit her labor room nurse. I tried to warn her, but the nurse just said, 'Oh, balls.' " We laughed, then looked guiltily at our children, because the word had fallen on their ears. "You should have seen the nurse when Michele went for her arm. I told you, I said . . ."

As they talked about their deliveries, I wandered from the den down a short corridor until I came to a bedroom. It contained a four-poster bed with a white gossamer canopy; the carpeting was a thick blue acrylic. On the desk sat Hal's picture, circled by a ring of rainbow carpeting, with the caption "Why is this carpet laughing?"

I picked up the phone and called Matthew at his studio. "I don't think I can take this."

"You mean the reunion?" he asked. I heard a baseball game in the background. "So go home."

"No, I mean us. Either you're with me or you aren't. If you're with me, then we have to do this kind of thing together."

Matthew sighed. "I'm doing the best I can."

"So what am I supposed to do?"

"Just be patient. Give me time."

"I can be patient about some things . . ." I wondered if it would always be like this. Me taking Bobby to birthday parties, helping him with his homework. "But when are you going to do anything about the birth certificate?"

"I don't know. I have a lot to think about."

"I want him to have a legal father. If anything happens to me, I want your name on the certificate."

"I've got to think about all of this," Matthew said again, with a sigh.

"Then call me when you have." My hand gripped the receiver. "But not before." I put down the phone, not exactly slamming it, but not cradling it either. My body shook. I was dressing Bobby to take him home when Michele, the woman who'd bitten her labor room nurse, came in. "I need to go. Matthew, I mean Jake, is coming home from Tokyo today." She seemed confused by my confusion. My life sounded so pathetic, even to me. "But you must stay," she said, "for the group picture."

"Oh, yes, the picture. Of course I'll stay for that." I took off the jacket I had just put on Bobby.

"So Jake couldn't make it," Michele said. There was something about her I liked.

"Actually Jake isn't my husband. It's a long story. We aren't married. I mean, I'm not married to anyone . . ."

"Oh."

"The baby's father, he didn't want the baby, not really. It was a mistake."

"The baby?"

"Oh, no, I don't mean having the baby was a mistake; I mean, it was an accident. It wasn't planned."

"But he might want the baby later on," she said, sounding very sympathetic.

"He might."

"But then you might not want him," she said with a smile.

"That's right," I said. "I might not want him."

It was time for the photo. We took our babies, all seven of them, and lined them up. These limp, loose forms who couldn't quite hold up their heads, bobbing like so many corks in the water, all on the sofa. I stuck Bobby at the end of the line, where he looked at me serenely as if he could make his way in a crowd, could already handle himself.

"Now smile," Irene and Hal said. Parents who'd brought cameras raised them, poised. Others jumped up and down, flapping their arms like birds. One child drooped and had to be pushed back up. The parents began again to wave frantically. This is where we will be forever as we send our children off on their first day at school, summer camp, their junior year abroad. We will always be these parents, left behind, bereft, smiling, waving.

"Say cheese," we shouted as the line of children began to collapse. "Say cheese." Lights flashed, children wailed. We rushed to them, propping them up before they fell.

THIRTEEN

I T WAS SHORTLY after my mother left that my father gave me the Night Sky. He'd gotten it in the gift shop on the desert road that sold things like cactus fertilizer and soil conditioners, owl rocks, rattlesnake eggs (rubber bands around a wire that made a rattling sound when opened), fool's gold, statues of tired prospectors, fake snakes that coiled, petrified wood with small carved animals on the top, dinosaur dung, rock concerts (rock animals with funny faces painted on them all glued together), and beautifully shaped stones with names like Apache tears, serpentine, fire agate. It also sold kits for the Night Sky, and for a long time I'd had my eye on one of them.

The shop was at the meteorite crater where I'd gone with my mother. I used to go inside when she was taking too long. They had a demonstration kit for the amateur astronomer with a paper telescope you could make yourself, a star chart with a circle you turn to follow the sky at the different seasons and times of the day, a booklet on all the constellations, and a clipboard where you could write down what you saw. It also had a small plastic bag filled with stars and as you spotted them in the sky, the kit explained how to put them on your ceiling. It promised that in the dark, your room would glow like the Milky Way.

After my mother left, my father began driving around the desert the way she had, looking for her, I think. She liked to go to all the sights, especially the ghost towns. She'd stare for a long time into shacks where cribs and ironing boards still stood, and get a dreamy look in her eyes as she envisioned warm hearths, happy homes. Maybe my father thought he'd find her and Sam in a ghost town. Or at the crater. Sometimes I think he went because he couldn't sit still. He just had to drive. His love of the desert bewildered me. I have always preferred the mountains and the sea, the vistas and the heights, but the spaces seemed to fill him.

Unlike my mother, my father wasn't partial to canyons, to big empty holes in the ground that made me feel as if I'd start falling and never stop. But after my mother was gone, he would stand at the edge, which made me very nervous, since he was all I had. I'd watch him and think, that's it for me. He's going to jump and there'll be no one to take care of me.

I had a friend at school named Buff who had dead eyes and lived in foster homes (one after the other), and I tried to imagine the foster homes I might live in. Some nice Mormon family where the girls wore purple eye makeup and everyone was so nice that it would terrify me. Or perhaps someone in the trailer park like Dottie would take me in. But then the state would take me away, saying I needed a proper home. I pictured myself in the hands of the law, with people asking, "Don't you have an aunt or an uncle somewhere? No next of kin?" They'd move me to California with religious fanatics who'd lock me in a closet when I was bad.

When my father took me with him to the meteorite crater, we'd stand at the rim of that giant pockmark, the wind blowing our hair flat against our heads, like two people who'd just made a successful landing on the moon. I'd look across the mile-or-so-wide crater and think I saw my mother, her tiny form, waving. He wouldn't walk the rim trail, for which I was grateful. Then we'd go into the souvenir shop. It was during one of those visits, when we were laughing, having forgotten who we were and why we'd come, that my father bought me the kit for the Night Sky.

He held it up. "Isn't this what you've been asking for? Isn't this what you want?" He looked at the plastic bag of stick-on stars. He looked through the paper telescope. Even though it was the middle of the day, a full moon was out and he focused on that. "You really can see." I looked, and in fact you could.

On the ride home, I took it apart. The telescope, the sky chart, the stars and planets for the ceiling. When we got home, my father helped me at first, but soon he lost interest, saying he had trouble figuring out where all the stars should go. I think he bought the kit to give me something to do while he was at work. I put it away for a while, because I wanted his help, but sometimes at night when I was alone and Dottie and her son, Jamie, weren't around, and I felt frightened by the night and by the fact that I was so alone in it and by all the things I did not understand, I would take it out and study the sky chart, the Amateur Astronomer's Guide. I put together a small scope, which felt cold when I pressed it to my eye. Once I understood how to translate what I'd seen in the heavens to what I could put on the ceiling of my room, I began to paste up the stars.

While my father went off on the night shift at the Glass Slipper—he arrived before it got really dark and was home by first light—I learned the constellations and licked stars to the ceiling. I began slowly with the Big Dipper and Orion, working my way up to Scorpio and Taurus. I'd take the telescope and study what there was to see. I measured carefully, charting my placements.

It was not long before the ceiling of my room glowed with golden stars, each carefully pasted; I hardly had to go outside at all to see the sky. It became a kind of obsession—the tracing of distances, the arrangements of the constellations. I'd mark the spots with pencils, and then glue on the stars. Sometimes I'd spend the entire night just tracing them from the moment my father left until I'd hear his car pull up.

After a few months I could turn out the lights and lie back on my pillow and see the Milky Way glowing over my head. I'd make wishes on the stars in my room, asking for a new bicycle or a move back to California. I never wished for their return. Instead, I wished for practical things, things that might have a chance of coming true.

FOURTEEN

IT WAS A WINDY DAY as I made my way down Broadway to the Chinese laundry where I'd dropped off some clothes three months before. I thought I'd be back in two or three days, but then Bobby came early and for a while I forgot about them. I couldn't even recall what I'd left there. Some shirts, cotton sweaters, a dress or two for spring. When I'd dropped the clothes off, I was preparing for a new season when the child would be here. Now it was months later. I couldn't find my ticket, though I looked everywhere—on my bulletin board, where I usually tacked such things, in pockets. But they knew me at the laundry. I'd been going there for years.

The wind blew across the West Side. Debris—dust, scraps of paper, fliptops—were in the air. I draped a cotton blanket loosely across Bobby's face, thinking I should go home. Save this for another day when I really needed whatever it was I'd left at the laundry. But this was what I'd planned to do. It was my outing for the day.

I walked a few blocks and noticed that Bobby was squinting, despite the blanket. I thought of pushing him backward, his face away from the wind, but instead I pulled the blanket higher. "It's all right," I said. "We're almost there." I looked at the list in my hand. The things I needed to get done. Groceries, stamps, a few art supplies, the laundry. Already I knew I'd have to pare it down.

At last I reached the laundry where for the past five years I had taken my things, except that now the laundry had a sign on the door: NO CARRIAGES ALLOWED. It didn't even say "please" or "sorry." Just this abrupt notice. I liked this laundry because it was especially good with stubborn stains like tomato or salad oil, and I seem to have a tendency to stain my clothes. I felt certain the sign wasn't there before, yet it looked yellow and torn. The tape was peeling around the edges.

I debated what to do. I thought of leaving Bobby for just a moment, keeping an eye on him through the window. But it didn't seem right with this wind. I could leave the stroller outside and carry Bobby in. Get the laundry, pay for it, carry it and Bobby outside, put him back. But my arms already ached from heaving him and his stroller up and down the stairs. It seemed too burdensome, so I decided to ask if I could, just this once, bring it inside.

I waved at the middle-aged Chinese woman whose store it was, the woman whose ancient mother, until she died, had hobbled on bound feet that made my heart go out to her. Now she smiled, waving back to me. Then I tapped on the glass, pointing to the carriage. Her smile faded, turning to a frown. She shook her head. She did not seem to recognize me even as I made a pleading sign with my hands, creating a sleeping pillow under my head, then pointing to the baby. She raised a finger, shaking it no.

Unsnapping Bobby, I lifted him into my arms, careful to bring the blanket with me. He groaned and let out a shout, because he was half asleep. "Don't worry," I said. "We'll go where there's no wind." I went in. The woman did not smile. She shouted something in Chinese to her thin, pimply son, who spoke English better than she did.

"I'm sorry," I explained, "but I can't find my ticket. You see, I had this baby and now, well, things are confusing, and I just can't find it."

He shook his head, pointing to the mountains of sheets, towels, men's shirts—parcels to the ceiling, neatly wrapped in brown paper. "Very busy," he said. "Not today."

"Slovak," I said, very precisely. "The name is Slovak."

The parcels were in chronological, not alphabetical order, so I tried to remember when I'd brought it in. "Eight weeks ago. Maybe more. Look down below."

Now Bobby began to howl. "Too busy," the man said. "Come back tomorrow."

I shook my head. "I'm sorry, I can't come back tomorrow. It's possible I can't ever come back again, so I'll just wait until you find it."

I sat on the windowsill. Bobby was still crying, hungry in my arms, so I opened my coat, pulled up my sweater, and began to nurse. I smiled at the young man and his mother, who looked at me in disgust, then turned away. "Don't hurry," I told them. "I'll wait."

The man now scurried up and down the ladder, pushing parcels aside, making room, finding nothing. At last near the top he found what he thought was mine. He tossed it down as I continued to nurse. When Bobby was done I examined the package. It was thin and did contain a few shirts, a pair of jeans I wouldn't fit into for a long time, my last links to the outside world. I gave the man twelve dollars and he handed me my change.

The breeze died down as I headed home, but it was getting late. I knew I should get Bobby home, yet I dreaded going there. Once I was inside, I was inside for good. Prisoners, invalids, mothers with newborns, we are all confined in this way. In an hour or so it would be dark, and then the only people I would see were the delivery boys who came and went, bringing me what I needed. Instead of going home, I decided to walk south to the post office. Maybe down to Shakespeare's to browse. Maybe I'd run into someone I knew.

I passed Pablo, my neighbor, who was walking his cat and dog bedecked in Easter bonnets. As I headed south, I looked at the faces in the crowd. Faces shielded from the wind. If Sam was among these people, I wouldn't be able to tell. The birthmark would be covered. Perhaps even my mother walked these streets, her face one I'd no longer recognize, riddled with age, for all the years that had gone by. Or would I? We went down Broadway, Bobby and I, with our faces in the wind, scanning the crowd. Then I saw, coming toward me, the woman who lived across the way. She was walking in my direction, her children trailing behind her.

Bobby fussed, and I stooped down to tuck his blanket round him. When I looked up, she was there, staring at me. She wore a teal blue jacket, which made her eyes all the more piercing. Her dark hair was pulled back in a ponytail, making her look severe, thin and drawn. I felt her bearing down as if she had something she wanted to say. "Hello," I said. I'm not sure why I said anything at all, but it seemed to be the right thing to do.

She looked annoyed, then surprised. "Hello,"

she replied with a questioning voice, as if she'd never seen me before.

"I live across the street from you," I said. "I work by the window. Maybe you've seen me there." I pointed back toward my street.

"Oh, yes," she said, like someone starting to wake up. Her eyes brightened for a moment and I saw her as I had years ago, when she was alive with possibility, young and very pretty. "Yes, I've seen you."

There was a pause, a long moment in which neither of us knew what to say. "I've just had a baby. Only a few months ago."

"Yes," she said, pondering my circumstances. "My husband left me around then," she said flatly.

"I noticed," I said. "I mean, I see things from the window when I work. I noticed that he was gone." There was another awkward silence. "What happened to the dog?" I said, realizing that I'd not seen her with a dog in some time.

"Oh"—she waved her hand as if swatting at a fly—"it was too much." She put her finger over her lips and whispered. "We gave him away."

I nodded somberly and found myself staring into her face, which close up was less pretty than from a distance. Her lines were more sharply drawn, her eyes set deeper than I had imagined. It was as if she had somehow sunk into herself. I looked away, down at her children. She held them with thin wrists, tiny bones I could have wrapped my fingers around. Her children tugged at her, and it seemed as if they would snap those bones in two.

There was something I wanted to say, but I wasn't sure what it was. I wasn't even sure why I had introduced myself. But because I had been watching her for so many years, I felt as if I knew her. As if I could say anything, though at the moment I was at a loss for words.

She looked at me oddly, uncertain of what was expected of her, then at Bobby, who squirmed. "You've dressed him too warmly," she said at last. I looked down at Bobby, in his flannel playsuit with a heavy sweater, the blanket still around him. "It's spring," she said. "He doesn't need all those clothes."

She was right. It had become warmer. I took the blanket away and unbuttoned his sweater. He smiled, grabbing at my fingers.

"My name is Mara," she said. "It's nice to meet you."

"My name is Ivy," I said.

She smiled. "Ivy." She repeated it as if she were remembering something. "It's a pretty name. Come over sometime," she said. "Come for a drink." And then she walked away.

FIFTEEN

EVERYTHING I DO is in doses. Measured restraint. Pieces at a time, as if I am fitting together a mosaic that is becoming more and more my life. A bit of reading, a snippet of conversation, a fragment of a film, a thought sliced like an onion. Memory is divided by feedings and wails. Cries in the night. Interruption has become a way of life: moments are cut into the portions of a pie.

I've been able to do more work at home. The Museum of Natural History has sent me some Native American pieces, and Mike has been sending me more projects than I can handle. He says we must be coming out of the recession because the jewelry business is back, and he seems to have plenty for me to do. "Stay home, Ivy," he tells me over the phone. "You get more done there." What he really means is that it's easier for everyone if I work at home.

For days at a time I don't go into the street. Whatever I need from the outside world I have sent to me, delivered by boys holding afterschool jobs. Chinese men with moist palms and no English appear at my door with steaming rice. Boys, earning their allowances, bring me videos at night. Hispanics now come for the laundry or drop off staples. Pizzas, Enfamil, bagels, entertainment; for the price of a tip, all this is brought to my door, to the door of a woman who was once accustomed to going anywhere at any time. The delivery boys eye me strangely, not with lust but with questions, as if I am a shut-in. Then they see the baby and they understand that this is true. I keep rolls of quarters by the door. Sometimes the only way I can be sure I am still in the world is the click the quarters make in their hands. I know them all by name. Tomás, Chen, Juan, LeRoy. The video store sends me either Jésus or Moses; I consider this to be a hopeful sign.

I have taken to watching mysteries late at night. Hitchcock, Christie, whatever I can order in. The man at the video store knows me and helps with my selections. "Mrs. Slovak," he says, hearing the baby crying in the background, "this one you won't be able to figure out." But I always do. The wife is the obvious suspect. Or the old friend. Or the husband trying to drive his wife insane. The lawyers who sleep with their clients; these I suspect right away. The red herrings, the twists of plot, the missing links; I know them. I am so good at this it frightens me, as if it's a calling I've missed, a talent, an activity I have a strange propensity for.

As I feed Bobby, a woman kills her husband with the frozen leg of lamb, then serves it to the detectives. They devour the murder weapon, the woman having brought off the perfect crime. What would I do under similar circumstances? I ask myself. The fact that I am asking at all has me concerned. When I have gone through the classics, the modern whodunits, what will feed my imagination? What will I invent to get me through?

Night after night, when I quit my work for Mike, I stare at the painting of the face that rises out of the mountains, against the desert; it has been on my work table for weeks. But by nine o'clock I collapse, too exhausted to paint.

One warm Saturday I took Bobby to the park. We went to Strawberry Fields, where I put him on a blanket in the sun. We sat beside two women, one with a newborn and the other in dark glasses with a toddler. The woman in dark glasses said, just as I sat down, "Let's face it, once you have a baby, that part of your life is over."

"What part?" I wanted to ask, but she was running across the field after her toddler. It was a warm, muggy day, unusual even for early May, and I stretched out on the blanket, staring up at the clouds, the trees overhead just beginning to blossom. When she came back, I heard her friend say, "What's the most embarrassing place for your water to break?"

"At an art opening . . ." the toddler's mother said, breathless from retrieving her child.

"Of your own work." Her friend laughed, patting her newborn. "That's where mine broke."

I found myself laughing as well, then longing for an opening of my own work. I would have been happy just to finish the painting on my desk. Restless, I put Bobby in his stroller and walked with him through the park. The pavement felt warm under my feet and I knew I wasn't ready for summer. I took him over to Diana Ross playground and put him in one of the infant swings. Holding him by the shoulders, I let him rock back and forth. Around me parents sat, talking while children dug into a sandbox. Others pushed children who pumped their legs frantically on swings. I rocked Bobby, back and forth, and felt as if I were in a time warp, slow action. I stayed here for a long time.

When I got home, I sat down to paint while Bobby took his nap. I looked at the picture and saw what I wanted to do. I wanted to deepen the lines around the face, make it recede farther into the picture. I wanted the road and the snake and the fence to look like snapshots or clippings from a magazine. The photorealist elements of the piece. I had begun to paint when Bobby woke. He was feverish, tossing. I gave him some Tylenol, but he stayed awake, fitfully, in my arms.

That night I dreamed I was in a room with a rat, a huge rat, and the rat was barring the door. Keeping me inside, threatening to bite.

When Jesús came over from the Video Connection with a horror film, I asked him to help me get down a box from the top of the closet; it contained my summer clothes. After he did this, he looked around. He saw the unmade bed, the pile of dirty clothes, a plate of half-eaten food. "Mrs. Slovak," he said after a long pause, "this place is kind of a mess." I stared at his face. He was young, perhaps not more than twenty, and he had olive skin and dark silky hair combed straight back.

I glanced around. "Yes, it is; I try to keep it together, but I've got so much to do."

"What about your husband? Does he work late?"

I smiled at Jesús. "I don't have a husband. That's why I can't get everything done."

He looked down at his feet. "You seemed kind of alone."

"I'm all right," I said. "Really I am." I wondered if he was going to leave or just stand there and stare at his feet.

"Well, if I can help you out again," he said, "just ask for me, or if you just want someone to share a slice of pizza and watch a good movie, let me know." I stood there, nodding like a wind-up toy, and pulled my robe tightly around me.

"I will," I said. "I'll let you know."

I offered him his usual tip, but he refused it. When I closed the door, I found myself slightly breathless. I thought of calling him back, but I didn't. Although I still wanted videos delivered, I knew I would stop calling for them.

After he left, I tried to watch the movie he'd delivered. But Bobby would not sleep. His eyes were fixed and black like my mother's when she was angry. Though I always thought his eyes and hair took after Matthew's, now it occurred to me that he looked like her. He started to cry. "Don't," I told him because tonight I didn't think I could handle it. I started eating a slice of vegetarian pizza and sipping a Diet Coke, though I knew this wasn't good for my milk. "Don't cry," I said, but he wouldn't stop. I was afraid that if I picked him up, I'd crush him.

He went red and stiff. I had to walk away. Then I wondered what his first memory of me would be. Of my back. Of me standing above him, a finger raised. My first memory of my own mother is fuzzy because I have so many memories of her, but they are not clear the way this one might be. I remember myself in a sink, my mother's black hair above me like a net about to drop on a wild animal. Or I see her at the window, her face pressed to the glass.

At last I walked over and picked him up, and he fell asleep in my arms. When he slept he was lighter than when he was awake. Lighter than air. I could have carried him forever when he was asleep. It was as if the spirit had abandoned the body, as if he had achieved weightlessness. Perhaps it is not the body that carries the weight. The body is mere gristle and bone. It is the spirit that weighs us down.

When I was certain he had settled down, I put him in his crib and went into the bathroom, but there was no toilet paper. I opened the refrigerator and found I had no juice, no milk. There was nothing for me to eat but the leftover pizza, and I was down to two diapers, barely enough to get him through the night. It was late, almost eleven o'clock, but the store on the corner was open. It wouldn't take long, fifteen minutes at most, for me to dash out and get just the necessities. No more. I could take Bobby with me, but it would mean waking him, getting him dressed, and it had taken so long to put him down.

Instead, I plugged in the nightlight in his room. It was a prism that cast a small rainbow on the wall. With my finger I traced its arc. Then I went into the kitchen and warmed a bottle. I placed a small stuffed giraffe beside Bobby's head and the warm nipple near his lips. On the cassette player I put on Brahms. Touching his brow to be certain he was asleep, I pulled the covers up to his chin, put on my coat, and headed out the door. I dashed down the stairs and into the street.

What could happen in fifteen minutes? He could wake up and put his head through the crib bars. A fire could break out in the electric socket in his room. He could wake up and be frightened to death. But sometimes it takes me five, ten minutes to reach his crib. I tried to imagine the night with no toilet paper, no juice, nothing to eat or drink. Not enough diapers. What are the chances of something happening if I went to the store? Infinitesimal. Hardly anything at all.

Three or four people were milling about in the corner store. It is run by Arabs, who are never very eager to do business. In their back room, they run a bookie operation. Here, men in kaftans make money change hands. They are never in a hurry. I began to grab things off the shelves—juice, milk, formula, diapers, butter, a bag of noodles, crackers, some Campbell's soup. The toilet paper and paper towels were up high, and I had to wait while the man at the counter rang up an order. Still he did not come, so I stood on a milk crate with a stick in my hand, batting away at the paper goods until they tumbled into my arms.

I raced to get in line, but a woman and drunk with a six-pack were ahead of me. He was fumbling with his change; he couldn't get the coins out. I looked at the clock. My heart was beating wildly. I never should have gone out. I should have wrapped Bobby and taken him with me; I should have waited until dawn. I'd been gone twelve minutes, and I was certain Bobby was awake. He's screaming. The neighbors have called the police; the police think—know—I am abusing my child. Child welfare is on its way to take my child away from me. They would be within their rights to do so. They are breaking down the door, and when I race up the street, arriving with the groceries in hand, they are standing there, ready to arrest me.

The drunk spilled a handful of change on the floor; he bent over, trying to pick up a quarter. His fingernails were dirty. A cigarette burned in his mouth. The woman in front of the drunk ordered a sandwich—salami and Swiss on rye with mustard and mayo and a pickle. How long would it take the proprietor to make her sandwich? Fifteen minutes have gone by. I should put my items back. The police are there; the child is dead. In just a matter of minutes, I have made the mistake I will pay for all my life.

"Excuse me," I pleaded with the woman. "My child is home alone. I need to hurry." Everyone looked at me with disdain. The woman, sizing me up, made a space with her hand and I moved to the head of the line. The man at the register, who knew me, said, "So where's the kid?" All eyes were upon me; everyone was ready to dial the police. "Asleep; a neighbor's watching him. But I've got to hurry."

He nodded. He didn't care if it was true or not. I paid quickly, fumbling, not unlike the drunk, with my bills, and dashed out the door. I ran up the street. It was eleven-thirty and I looked to see if flames leaped from my window, if the rescue squad had arrived. But the building was quiet. There were no screams. As I slipped inside, my downstairs neighbor, a closet homosexual who speaks lovingly in Greek with his mother on the phone, was coming in with a male companion. "So," he said, "how's it going?" Always the same friendly smile. Upstairs I heard the laughter of the two girls who sublet the apartment across from mine from the actress who has yet to make it big on the West Coast.

I turned the key—and was greeted by darkness and quiet. Not a sound. Half-expecting to find Bobby gone, I raced to the crib. He lay on his back, his chest rising and falling. I collapsed on my bed, exhausted, and fell into a deep sleep. But it was not long before I heard Bobby's cry. "Please," I heard myself saying, "please, not now."

Toward the end my mother would interrupt my sleep. She'd come into the room while Sam and I slept. We had been tucked in by our father, who told us stories about a black swan with heavy wings that took us to a land of chocolate lakes and gumdrop mountains. But she'd come in and shake us, bringing us abruptly back. Her hair hacked off, short, hideous. Her features pinched, fierce.

She came to us first with her dreams. Dreams of empty houses, no one there. Dreams of missing people and strange beasts. Her breath smelled of cigarettes as she shouted into our sleep, her sadness turned to rage. "Do you know what it's like for me, living here? I come from Pennsylvania. My family had money. We lived in a big house." Often she was naked, her body trembling. The first few times it happened, I thought the house was on fire and we had to flee. "I was somebody else," she'd shout. "I was somebody before." She'd wake us four times a night, then not at all for a week. She shook us until our father staggered in and led her away. For years I never really slept, feeling that at any moment I could be awakened.

Now I lay, listening to Bobby's cry. "Please, don't," I pleaded with my infant son. "Please, don't wake me again."

I picked up the phone and called Tucson. I was relieved when Dottie answered, her voice groggy with sleep and thick with her cigarettes. "It's me," I said. "It's Ivy."

"What is it? My God, what time is it where you are?" I heard the rustle of sheets, the flattening of a pillow. My father's voice was muffled. "Who is it, Dot? Who's calling at this hour." She shushed him. "It's Ivy."

"What's wrong?" I heard my father say. Tears filled my eyes.

"I'm going to put the baby up for adoption," I told her. "I can't take it anymore."

"Don't, Ivy." She sounded frightened. "Promise me you won't."

"I can't promise. I made a mistake."

"Send her a plane ticket home," my father said. He grabbed the phone away. "Either I'll come there or you come here. Those are your choices. Period," he said. I knew he meant it.

Somehow I didn't want anyone going anywhere. I didn't know what I wanted. "Don't do it," Dottie said. "You'll regret it all your life." She knew what she was talking about. "We'll send you money for a baby sitter, a plane ticket, we'll take the baby for a few months, whatever you want."

I thought of them out there in the desert. The cactus, the miles of white sand. My father got on the phone.

"You're not a quitter," he said. "That's not the Ivy I know. You know, I folded the laundry and cooked for you for all those years. It wasn't easy, but I did what I had to; that's all."

"I know you did, Dad." I could see him at the Laundromat, the racing page on his lap, his pockets full of dimes for the machines. "I've been thinking about her lately," I said.

"Don't waste your time, Ivy."

"I've been thinking about why she left."

"Forget the ones who left," he said, his voice filled with irritation. "Think about the ones who stayed."

There was silence. This had always been his point. At last I said, "But maybe I'm like her."

"You aren't."

"How do you know?"

"Because you think about it, because it worries you." His voice rose as he spoke. "Your mother never thought about anything . . . except herself."

"Lately I seem to remember everything."

"The only thing you need to remember is that Dottie and I love you very much. We love you and we love Bobby. And we're proud of you."

"I can't work," I said. "I can't get anything done. Did you ever think"—I was trying to keep from crying—"did you ever think about giving me up? When things were difficult?"

He paused. There was a long sigh. "Sure, I thought about it. Given my situation, I would've been crazy not to think about it. But thinking about it and doing it are two different things. You were my daughter, Ivy. You always will be."

Now the tears were running down my cheeks. "Thanks, Dad. I'll be all right."

"I know you will," he said, his voice cracking. "You'll be fine."

SIXTEEN

MY STEPMOTHER'S NAME was Dorothy, but my father called her Dot, which only served to remind me in the early years of how small and insignificant she was in our lives. I called her Dottie from the start because she asked me to, though in my teens I began to call her Mom. Because she also had red hair—though hers came from a bottle—most people assumed she was my mother and almost no one asked.

Once, however, a teacher during a conference asked me in front of my parents where I got my brown eyes, and I replied, "From my mother." The teacher stared at Dottie, with her brilliant blues, then at my father, then back at my chocolate browns. "From her mother's side," my father said.

Three years after my real mother left, my father divorced her *in absentia* and married Dottie. He did it for me; I knew that. But when he married her, I ran away from home. I'm not even sure what came over me, because I knew Dottie well and I even cared for her. But the day they went down to the Hitching Post on the Strip, I packed a small bag with some clothes, a baloney sandwich, several Nancy Drew mysteries, and left. I got a ride first with a drunk who was hauling pigs. When I couldn't stand the smell of him or the truck, I asked him to let me out, and he put his hand on my thigh. I was ten years old, but I shoved his hand away. I thought he was going to kill me. Instead, he told me to get out of his truck.

The next guy who picked me up had a truck-load of grapes. On the seat beside him he had bunches of green and purple grapes. His fingers were purple from plucking them. He was very fat, with snakes tattooed up and down his arms. The grapes must have been sprayed with pesticides, because I itched all over and my eyes burned. I think when I fell asleep he radioed the troopers, because they came and got me when we were at a truck stop having a Coke. He gave me a key chain with a little truck on it. I still use it for my keys.

When the troopers brought me back, my parents wept. Dottie was still wearing her apricot wedding gown and was putting out cigarettes into platters of uneaten cold cuts. I thought they were going to hit me, which they never had, but instead they embraced me as if I were some blessed being and not a runaway kid.

"The first time I ever laid eyes on Ivy Slovak," Dottie often said, "it was like she was on fire. Wild eyes, burning red hair. And there was something else about her—like she'd explode with the tiniest spark. It was left to me to tame her."

Dottie told this to anyone who asked about us. She seemed to love telling it, whether I was in the room or not. It was how she explained herself and everything around her. "First I took care of the girl," she said with a laugh. "The father came later."

My mother and Dottie used to sit for hours in the late afternoon on the plastic lawn chairs, smoking cigarette after cigarette. Dottie usually had her hair in brush rollers. (She never wore them to sleep because Ralph wouldn't let her, she confided in my mother with a suggestive cackle that came back to me after Ralph died, even after my father and Dottie were together.) Ralph dealt poker, though he wasn't a gambler, not like my father. It was just what he did. He was a simple man, not good at much, but he loved his family. He died of throat cancer before he reached forty.

Ralph and Dottie had a boy named Jamie. Jamie and I used to take off our clothes and display our private parts to each other for hours, but no one seemed to notice. Later, when we were adolescents and stepbrother and stepsister, this would embarrass us so much that we had difficulty being in the same room. Jamie was fair, with blue eyes like his mother, and two years my senior. He turned out to be a relatively successful management consultant and now lives with his wife and two children out west.

My mother and Dottie would sit up in the evening, smoking, sipping Cokes, talking about what it was they imagined their lives would have been if they'd done things differently. In those years Dottie had a nice Airstream, and they lived in it through several states, but mostly in Reno and Vegas. Jamie had been born in that trailer. So my mother and Dottie talked about their lives and about what would have happened if they hadn't married and had children. How they would have become models or dancers or whatever it was they thought they wanted to be. At times I think Dottie felt guilty, as if somehow she'd planted ideas in my mother's head, seeds that had given her the idea to run away, but I always told Dottie this wasn't true. Even before she met Dottie, my mother was gone.

It was Dottie who saved me. "I began with food," she said. "Cooking things kids just can't say no to, like fried chicken and hot dogs, grilled cheese, and thick malteds you eat with a spoon. My own mashed potatoes and biscuits. Not that her father didn't feed her; he did. He just didn't make the things children love." From food she moved on to schedules. A time to get up, a time to eat, to study, to take a bath. Everything for Dottie was done by the clock. "Ivy," she'd say, "it's six-thirty; you should be doing your homework now."

Dottie didn't move in right away. It was a process that took place over many months. First there was Jamie to think about, and then there was me. And of course Dottie was not stupid, and living with my father had its drawbacks. I'm not sure, even now, how she put up with it, because we all knew that if my mother walked in the door, even years after she had gone, he'd have taken her back.

Shortly after Dottie came to live with us—which was about two years after my mother was gone—she told me the story about the child she had given away. When Dottie got pregnant by her childhood boyfriend in the rugged farming community where she'd grown up, outside Bakersfield, the boy acted as if he didn't know what she was talking about. In fact, they had been making love in the back seat of his father's pickup since they were fourteen. During her pregnancy the boy didn't seem to know her. Dottie gave up the little girl when she was three days old and thought that was the end of it.

But one day five years later the boy, who was now a grown man with a family of his own, phoned in tears to say that the people who had adopted their little girl had given her back. He sobbed as he spoke, begging Dottie to forgive him. He told her that the child was defective somehow and the people had returned her, the way you would a car that was a lemon. He knew this because a friend of his family heard about it, but they didn't know where the child had been taken.

Whenever Dottie spoke of the girl she'd given away, and then of her years going from orphanage to orphanage in eastern California, trying to track her down, I'd curl against her body and let her stroke my hair. Dottie would lie with me and smoke, blowing thin blue circles around my head. "Ivy, I'm glad I found you," she'd say, "because you've come to replace the one I gave away." I was like a gift, she told me, that had been given back to her, and I had to admit that I felt as if I'd been found.

Sometimes when she tucked me in, I'd ask her to tell me the story again. I made her tell me about the pleading faces of children, their trembling lips, hands that held her. About the ones who ran to her and said, "Mommy, Mommy, please take me home."

SEVENTEEN

THE APARTMENT needed to be fumigated. "Pests," the landlord said. The whole building was infested. He suggested that I go away for a few days, stay with friends. They would spray on Friday, and I could return after the weekend. I called Patricia at her office, and she said, somewhat hesitantly, that I could stay at her place. I decided to visit museums and see some special exhibits, something I'd been wanting to do anyway, until Patricia got home from work.

The exterminators were coming at around ten, and I wanted to be out before they arrived. But first I had to feed and dress Bobby. I nursed him early and laid out his clothes. I wanted to shower, so I pulled his portable crib near the bathroom and turned on the mobile. It would play for five minutes, enough, I hoped, for me to jump into the shower. I could hear him cooing, then fussing.

"Mommy's coming," I called. "Mommy will be right there!"

The water felt good as it poured over me, hot and relaxing. I closed my eyes and thought that I could stay there a long time. My body, which had been dormant, seemed to wake, and I ran my hands over its length. It was weeks since I'd told Matthew I wouldn't see him until he signed Bobby's birth certificate. But now as I tilted my head, letting the water flow over my face, the thought of him came back to me. I could walk out of the shower, and he'd be there, sitting on the bed, aroused. Or, perhaps, impatient for me, he'd open the bathroom door, pull back the shower curtain. He'd take off his clothes and join me, soapy hands coursing over my skin.

The mobile stopped and Bobby began crying, so I leaped out, covered in suds. Giving the mobile a twist until the plastic giraffe, elephant, and dog turned again to the tune of "It's a Small World," I jumped back in the shower to rinse off. When I got out, Bobby was pounding his fists into the mattress. I took off his diaper, and a stream of urine rose, stinging my eyes so that I could not see.

Wet, naked, with burning eyes, I pinned Bobby to the table and grabbed the towel on my head to wipe my face. I hummed a song my father used to sing, about poor little lambs who'd lost their way, but it was no use. He was in a rage, so I nursed him again, wondering what the exterminators would think when they arrived. Greedily he sucked at my breast.

At last he grew still, and I raced to fill a small duffel with the changes of clothes we'd need for the weekend. I packed only a few toys. A rattle, a plastic teething ring. A book whose pages were soft, like the fur on a bunny. A sketch pad and novel for me. I could stick this duffel under the seat of the stroller or strap it around the back. Then I filled Bobby's diaper bag with bottles, soft blankets, as many diapers as could fit. I tried to remember which museums permitted strollers and which ones made you rent a backpack or use a Snugli. I didn't want to use the Snugli, because Bobby's weight made my shoulders ache and because I needed to carry all those other things, but I stuffed it in anyway. The Met and the Modern both permitted strollers on off-peak times, so I decided to make my way to the Met.

I still had to dress Bobby. The flannel playsuit I tried to put him in was too small; the top barely closed. The bottoms rode up at his ankles. Reaching down into the changing table drawers, I pulled out other playsuits, a cotton running suit, pajamas, but they were all the same size. He'd outgrown the presents he'd received when he was born. Already I'd have to buy him new things.

I found a playsuit slightly bigger than the others, but as I started to put it on, he began to cry. "There, now, hold still." I wished there were someone I could hand him to, someone who would dress him, clean him, brush his hair, and give him back to me when it was all done. Once again I found myself wondering what had ever made me want this child or made me think I could handle him alone. Again, it seemed that I could crush him with my hands. Instead, I held him down firmly with one hand as I struggled to pull his pants up with the other.

It was a rainy day, and we headed to the cross-town bus. At the bank I stopped to get cash for the weekend. I withdrew fifty dollars and saw on the slip that I had about five hundred in checking and a thousand or so in savings. I figured we could survive for another two months with that and the money I was earning from Mike, but then I'd need to start making a real living. And I'd have to hire someone to watch Bobby.

At the bus stop the wind whipped my legs while Bobby banged his fists into the plastic rain cover. His face looked distorted as he pounded. No bus was in sight. I tapped on the outside and together we banged our fists until he began to smile, then laugh. For a few moments we played the punching game, both of us laughing.

Suddenly the bus pulled up and the driver opened the door. Others went on as I stood, struggling. I managed to get Bobby out of the stroller, but I couldn't fold it up because of the rain cover. Impatient New Yorkers glared at me, shaking their heads. The bus driver, a dark man with tired features, watched. I saw him swallow a pill. "You can go ahead," I said. "I can't get this thing to fold up." The driver sighed.

He put his bus in park, got out of his seat, pushed people out of the way. He grabbed the stroller and carried it onto the bus. I clutched Bobby in one arm and the bag with our belongings in the other. Once on board, I fumbled with my change, dropping I don't know how much money into the machine, and looked for a seat, only to find there was none. I stood balancing stroller, baby, the shoulder bag, and myself precariously against a pole. Then the driver blared, "We are not moving until the woman with the baby has a place to sit." A man rose, a sea parted as I made my way into the seat, which was reluctantly offered.

Faces stared down at me. Faces filled with fatigue or pity. Faces disgusted or wistful, etched with desire or the end of desire. The businessman with a scowl, the young woman with a blank look, the older woman in black who smiled at the baby. As the bus wound its way across town, my eyes closed, I fought to stay awake. What would happen if I did fall asleep? What if I dashed off the bus, about to miss my stop? I recalled the Lichtenstein image with the caption "Oh, God, I left the baby on the bus." I could see how this might happen. You're weighed down. You're carrying too much. It's one more bundle, after all.

Or you go to a party, get drunk, leave the child asleep on your friend's bed. You don't notice him, sleeping there beside the pile of coats. You just forget, slip back into your former life, the life you had when there was just one person, not two or, for most people, three. How far would you get before you realized you'd left the party without your child? Out the door? Down the stairs? To the house of the man who was taking you home? The next day? Once, I read about a woman in Florida who put her baby in the car seat on the top of the car, packed the car for a vacation, then drove away with the baby on top. The baby was all right, but the mother—would she ever be the same again?

I managed to get the stroller folded just as the bus was coming to the corner of Seventy-Ninth and Fifth, where I had to get off. I pushed the buzzer for my stop and quickly made my way down. With Bobby in my arms and the rain coming down hard, I struggled to open the stroller. Bobby squirmed, trying to get his face out of the rain.

At last I tucked him in, though I didn't bother to strap him, since we were only going across the street. I prayed he wouldn't slip out. When we reached the Met, I didn't see the elevator for the handicapped, so I carried the buggy up the steps. Inside the checkroom the attendant glanced at me and said, "If you are planning to see any special exhibits, you must check your stroller." I groaned.

I wanted to see the Impressionist exhibit, which included pieces from private collections that had never been seen before, so I had no choice but to check. I deposited everything but the baby and his diaper bag. Then I put Bobby down on the bank of seats and tucked him into his Snugli, where he went to sleep.

Slowly I made my way up the grand staircase. At the top I turned left, toward the exhibition hall, and found myself in a room of paintings of the early Christian martyrs and saints.

I was interested in the faces of those in pain, the expressions of the suffering. The martyred with arrows piercing their breasts, thorns cutting into their skulls. The saint standing in a boiling pot, being flayed alive. In each, the look of serenity affirmed that the suffering of the body could not touch the soul.

There was something in the eyes that I wanted to capture, to reproduce. I had never quite seen it in this way before, but now I did. Those placid, questioning eyes turned upward. A look I had seen in the eyes of the homeless, the impoverished, the desperate. Fumbling in my purse, I found a pencil and a small notepad and I began to draw, my arms wrapped around my baby's head.

I wandered through the galleries, moving from the Middle Ages to Byzantium, then coming out slowly through the Renaissance, and I was about to go into the Nineteenth Century when Bobby woke up. He began to fuss, so I found one of the two restrooms in the Met, where a line snaked along the wall. Though stalls were emptying, the line was long. A group of frail old women wearing little name tags was resting against a wall. There were young mothers with children jumping up and down, clearly in need of going to the bathroom. Behind me was a pregnant black girl who could not have been more than sixteen. When I was pregnant, I had seen them—black, white, Hispanic—still children, really, round as basketballs, about to have children of their own. This girl swayed back and forth, sighing, her bladder about to burst as she rubbed her aching back. I turned and she looked at me, then at Bobby, with inscrutable eyes. I told her to go ahead. I was waiting for one of the handicap stalls.

I'm not sure when I began using the handicap stalls, but it was before I got pregnant, before Bobby was born. When I got pregnant, of course, it made sense, because I was large and, toward the end, felt looming. And with Bobby it made sense, because being with a small child was a kind of handicap. People held doors for you (or they were supposed to); they gave you their seats. They lifted things you couldn't lift. And with Bobby in bathrooms where there were no changing tables, I had to change him with his head dangling in the sink and in front of makeup mirrors, where women stared at his often erect penis and testicles—for I must say that he was born well-endowed, as if his manhood were somehow already formed. I had changed him on the floors of museums and restaurant bathrooms, wondering what diseases he would pick up. Little girls peered down; other mothers grinned knowingly. Yes, their nods told me, I know what this is. I've been there.

It was the space I liked in the handicap stalls, space I missed elsewhere. The way you could stretch out, not get your purse and bags and coat all bunched up in a tiny cubicle. Often I was loaded down with art supplies, cameras, purchases I'd made (I was always making purchases, little things—socks, mittens from street merchants, those men with foreign accents who shouted "Gloves, four dollars" on the street). Sometimes I would splurge and buy food I could not really afford—pumpkin tortellini at Fairway, a certain walnut bread in SoHo.

Perhaps it all began when I was trying to please Matthew, bringing him what I thought he'd like. A comforter if the weather suddenly turned. A pastry he loved. Or, when I could afford it, which wasn't often, a free-range chicken from the Jefferson Market. Why I felt I needed to please him at all was a mystery to me; I didn't really think about this until after he was gone. Matthew seemed to like everything. In fact, he liked everything equally. He liked flowers or no flowers, walnut bread or Wonderbread. He liked to be warm, but he never minded being cold. He liked a new sweater or no sweater at all.

People always said—people who worked with him, like his assistant Walter, or friends like Patricia and Scott, or Jake—that Matthew was easy to get along with. No one doubted that. He was an easy person to be with. Our friends also said to me sometimes when we were having trouble, and especially toward the end, that Matthew was a difficult man to know. He was easy, but he was unknowable. And now I was trying to decide whether this was true. It wasn't only that I was trying to please him that made me weigh myself down with so many packages and use the handicap stalls. I wanted to see him react. What if I came home with black hair, my red locks cut off, would he say something? Would he notice?

It had all burdened me. Loaded me down with boxes, packages, small items. So I'd stop by museums and use the handicap stalls. I'd wait patiently while old women in diapers made their way into the special stalls. I listened as arthritic limbs settled down. Listened to the groans of the elderly trying to pee or defecate as sagging sphincters, weakened limbs, swollen joints refused. Or I'd watch children in wheelchairs, damaged at birth, children who struck terror into me when I was pregnant, children who had not gotten the oxygen they needed, whose spines had been twisted in the birth canal, whose hips had been snapped from the sock-

ets. Children whose brains and limbs had been ad-
dled before they knew what it was to have them.

Once I'd wondered who the group was that had
lobbied for the ramps and special entranceways.
Access was their word. The alternatives to revolv-
ing doors. The buses that dropped low to the pavement. The bathroom stalls I'd used first out of a
sense of spaciousness, then out of necessity. When
was it that I began to need the ramps, the special
entranceways—that I had joined the ranks of the
invalids?

Patricia's apartment was filled with good antiques
—both English and American. She had chests of
cherrywood and pine and a maple hutch that held
the china she had registered at the best shops when
she became engaged to Scott, years before I met
them. She was the only person I knew who had
real silver. In her kitchen hung shiny copper pots
without a trace of tarnish. Everything about her
house was ordered, regulated, neat. And shimmering. How impeccably she ran her life, as if this
sense of order was her greatest source of pride.

Patricia stood at the sink, chopping broccoli and
carrots, while Scott sat in the living room in front
of the TV, headphones on, remote in hand, flip-
ping channels. She gave me a hug, poured me seltzer with lime, and told me to make myself at
home. "You'll sleep in the living room. You and
Bobby can sleep together, right?"

"Sure," I said. "Listen, I really appreciate this. I mean, I'm grateful for your letting me stay here."

"Oh, it's no problem. Just make yourself comfortable. How are you? How was your day?"

I began to describe it to her. The early morning struggles to leave the apartment, the exhaustion of just getting to the Met. "But then it all changed. I don't know. Wandering through the museum, being out for the day. I felt very . . ." I didn't know what I wanted to say, but I noticed that Patricia didn't seem to be listening. She was chopping vegetables, preparing dinner. "Well, it made me feel better. As if I could start to do things again. Do you understand?"

She smiled but said nothing.

"So," I said, deciding to change the subject, "what's the crime this week?"

Patricia hesitated. "Well, it isn't exactly a crime. It's a tragedy, really. It came over the wires this morning. At first the police thought there might be foul play. In California a woman's car stalled on the railroad tracks. Her three children were in the car. They were very small and a train was coming. So the woman leaped out of the car and tried to flag the train down. But it couldn't stop in time."

"My God!" I said. "That's terrible!"

"It's so sad, isn't it? I can't imagine how that poor woman must feel."

I shook my head and looked at Bobby, who was awake, smiling. It wasn't a crime, that was true, but somehow the story didn't sound right. I felt as if Patricia were telling me a riddle, and I've never been good at solving riddles. "I don't know," I said. "Something's not right about it."

"How can you say that?"

I shrugged. "I just know that something's wrong."

Patricia looked at me, her face set hard, as if she were blaming me for something I didn't do. "The woman was distraught," she said. "It couldn't be helped. That's what the police decided."

Unsettled by the story, puzzled by what felt like a missing piece, and not wanting to get into an argument with Patricia, I took Bobby into the living room to change him. The news was over, and Scott had a basketball game on. He was also playing a video game in his lap. Bugs Bunny scrambled to eat a carrot. Five carrots and he won. Scott pecked away at it until dinner was served, gleeful whenever he won.

We ate steamed vegetables, brown rice, fish, while listening to a CD of Brahms. Scott kept one eye on the basketball game—Lakers versus the Celtics—he had not turned off, though there was no sound. Patricia had a rule about television. He could watch it, but she didn't want to hear it. "So," Scott said, his eyes wincing at a bad play, "have you been getting back to work?" Then he grimaced; another play had gone awry.

"A little. I'm going to have to do something soon. Money's getting tight."

"Well, what about Matthew? Can't you hit him up for some?"

"Scott," Patricia said angrily, "we've discussed this. You know what the situation is."

"Pretty rotten, if you ask me."

"It was my choice," I muttered.

"Still pretty rotten." Scott hit his fist against the table. A jump shot had succeeded.

"Big game, huh?"

"Big game, little game," Patricia said. "He watches them all."

Suddenly, after dinner, I realized how tired I was. I had walked a great deal that day and been out for hours. And besides, I could think of nothing to talk about. If I went to bed, I'd feel better in the morning. Reluctantly, Scott turned off the television and went into their room. Patricia opened the sofa bed. There was something official about her movements, as if I were a renter in a boarding house. She brought in some sheets and towels.

"Will he cry?" she asked, putting a pillow case on the pillow.

"I beg your pardon?"

"Will he cry in the night?"

"Do you mean will he wake you up?"

Patricia looked chagrined. "It's Scott. He has trouble if he's awakened in the night. He has trouble going back to sleep."

"So do I."

Patricia smiled weakly.

"But no," I said, "I don't think he'll cry, or if he does, I'll nurse him quickly so he won't disturb you or Scott."

Rage welled up within me as I watched Patricia turn to go into her room. "Anyway, I'll be leaving in the morning. You don't have to worry about me. I'll be out early."

"Ivy, that isn't necessary . . ."

"I'm sorry I came here," I said, voice cracking. "I really didn't know where else to go."

EIGHTEEN

THE FIRST WINTER after my mother and
Sam disappeared, a toddler who lived not far
from us wandered outside while his father, who
perhaps had been drinking, slept. The night the
boy wandered off, we had a cold snap. Most people
don't think of the desert as being cold, but a fierce
wind can come from the north, the kind that
cracks your skin. When the man's wife came home
(she worked the night shift at a coffee shop in one
of the casinos), she found the door open. She had
no idea how her husband had slept through that
cold. They searched for hours for the boy and
found him, frozen, a mile from his home. That's
how far he'd wandered. When my father heard
this, he said, "Don't ever go out if I'm not here."
He shook his finger at me. "Don't ever go out
alone."

Yet my father still went off on his own. I begged

him to stay with me, but he'd say, "I can't. I can't sit here and do nothing." He never spoke of what had happened with my mother and Sam. He just got restless; he moved around like a hyperactive child. A gambler has what they call "tells." The way he pulls at his chains, turns his ring. Runs a finger through his hair. With my father, it was the pacing.

He tried to sit in front of the television, but soon his leg bounced into the air, his hand tapped the desk. Then he'd be up and pacing, and soon he'd say, "I'm sorry, honey, but I've got to go somewhere. I'll be back soon. You know I will." And he went out. I'd stand on the steps of the trailer, watching his red hair. I got my red hair from my father, only his covered his whole body. After my mother and Sam left, he began to slouch. On the nights when he walked away, my father looked like an orangutan, and this thought sometimes made me laugh.

He'd pause at the street and wave. "Whatever I win tonight, it goes to you." I'd smile and shake my head. He was going down to Glitter Gulch, the skid row of Vegas, where he'd play poker with the tourists—the polyester crowd in their powder-blue doubleknits and pompadours, the women in tangerine and lime pants suits. Here he'd mostly win. And then he'd go on to the high-stakes card games, the ones behind closed doors, and here he'd lose.

Then I was just a child alone in a trailer park. Sometimes Dottie came over. She'd bring me a pot of stew. But mostly, on the nights my father left, I'd do housework, dusting or ironing his shirts, though he asked me to stop after a while because of the yellow marks I left.

When I was done with the housework, I'd sit in front of the television, watching shows like "Leave It to Beaver" or "Life With Father." I'd fall asleep in the chair and stay there until my father wrapped his arms around my legs and carried me, fireman's style, into my room. On those nights, when I was alone and my father came home late, all his winnings went to me. I'd wake in a daze as he dropped coins into my hand. "For your college fund," he'd say. I kept the coins in a box. I had three hundred dollars when it was time for me to go to college.

One night when he came home at dawn and found me in the chair, I put my arms around his neck and pulled him down to me in a breathless embrace, as if I could not let go. "What do I do if you don't come home?" I whispered into his ear. "What happens to me?"

"Nothing's going to happen to either of us," he said, but his voice sounded shaky, as if he weren't quite sure.

There was a woodpile around the side of the trailer, and I used to play there when my father was gone on a Saturday or Sunday afternoon. I stacked the wood and made small forts. I piled it for hours, warding off imaginary assaults. One afternoon when my father came home, he found me at the woodpile and asked, "Are you having fun? Are you having a good time?" He saw a small black speck on my arm and went to flick it away, but his finger sank into my flesh as if it were made of custard. We both stood, staring into the gaping hole, like a sink hole, growing larger and larger, though I felt no pain at all. At first he thought I'd poured acid on my skin. Then he began to cry and he picked me up and raced to the car. I gripped the door handle as he sped through red lights.

My father carried me into the emergency room, though I felt well enough to walk. He kicked the door open with his foot. The doctor took my arm. The nurse hurried to bring him the syringe he'd asked for. They are tiny things, those spiders, only a quarter of an inch long. But their bite can kill a child. My father sat, sobbing, holding my hand. The white-coated doctor patted his back. "She'll be all right," he said as he gave me the injection. "She'll be fine." But still my father sobbed.

When the spider bite was still raw on my arm, we left Vegas because of a gambling debt my father could not pay. It was summer and there was no school, so I wasn't missing anything yet. We were regrouping, my father said. He did odd jobs to pay off the debt. When he went out during the day, he took me with him. We'd get into the pickup and go to a small shop or someone's garage, where my father moved wires around. He fiddled with the insides of things until he made them work. There was almost nothing he could not make right.

We hardly discussed my mother and Sam's leaving, but often we talked about them as if they were still there. My father believed that someday they'd be back, that they hadn't left for good. I think he was so accustomed to my mother's little excursions into the desert—a day here, two days there—that he thought they'd gone on an extended one. He'd say things like "Your mother would love this shop" or "Sam would think this is the greatest grilled cheese." But we never talked about what mattered. About the things that might have enabled me to get on with my life.

My father never liked to talk about the past—his own especially. "What's done is done," he said if anyone asked him where he'd been. But on the road as we traveled that summer and the tedium of driving took over, he told me bits and pieces of his life. He was just a boy, the youngest of seven, when he emigrated from Poland with his older brother, Max. In London they slept on park benches until one night someone hit them on the head with a bottle. My father still hears a ringing in his ear. Eventually they made it to New York, and tried to bring the rest of the family over. But

Hitler had already marched into Poland. By 1940 the letters from home stopped.

About my mother he remained silent, and I suppose I never asked. Then one night we checked into a motel and after dinner he put a bottle of bourbon down, which he didn't do often. He had aged since we'd found them gone a little over a year before. His thick head of coppery hair had thinned and he looked tired and worn. Deep lines furrowed his brow, the corners of his eyes. As the bourbon got lower and lower, he began to talk about my mother, and I listened as if I were being told a fairy tale. It was as if in explaining her to me he was explaining her to himself as well. "When I met your mother," he told me, "she was the most beautiful woman I'd ever seen. But more than that, there was something about her. Something that looked"—he searched for the right word—"terrified." She had intrigued him. "Jessica told me many things," he went on. He'd never before referred to her by name, and it made me feel that somehow, definitely, she was gone. "I'm still not sure what is true."

My mother, he said, came from a mining town in Pennsylvania, though she claimed for years to have come from wealthy Philadelphia stock. In one version her father was the scion of a rich blueblood family and had married the Italian maid. In another her mother had been a flamenco dancer. Once she'd made a convincing case for her mother's having been a fine painter of portraits. He had tried to track her family down—and I tried myself years later—but he found nothing. "I feel pretty certain," my father told me that night, "that Jessica invented her life." But she was beautiful, he said, and exotic, and he hadn't really cared. One thing in all of her stories was consistent, though. Her father had been an abusive man, capable of cruelty, and her mother drank to forget, and no one paid Jessica much heed. "You know what I think," my father said. "I think they were simply mean-spirited people and Jessica's beauty went to her head. It was her way out."

When she turned seventeen, she saved for a train ticket to Hollywood and she never returned. She worked as an extra in films. That was where she met my father before she was twenty years old. It seemed only right that these two people whose pasts had been obliterated—my father's by history, my mother's by her own will—should come together in the late 1940s, adrift, without families, working in the motion picture industry. One night when I was grown, I went to see an old film in which my mother was an extra—an Indian squaw, dancing wildly around a campfire.

That fall when I started school outside Reno, I told people that my father was a cartographer, which was why we moved around so much. They were always interested in what I said my father did. I said he was assigned by the U.S. Army

Corps of Engineers to make maps across the Southwest. His specialties were mountains, desolate terrain, the kind of places most mapmakers hate to tackle. No people, no roads, no significant landmarks. Endless vistas, pure topographical complexities.

In those dried-up desert towns, I learned to become a fairly accomplished teller of tales, not unlike my mother, I suppose, and people believed me. They envisioned him out there, surveying the land, determining distances, and I found it also interested me. My stories about him grew quite elaborate. He became a man who loved borders, having done both the Mexican and Canadian. He had done Alaska and Texas, two difficult states. I described for students in my new school what it was like living in the Alaskan wilderness—the freezing mornings, the pristine skies, the ambling polar bears. I made up elaborate nonsense about living on seal fat, and no one doubted a word I said.

The teacher, Miss Willenford, finally asked if my father could come and talk to the class about his mapmaking career. Tell how he got into the business, what he looks for when he studies a landscape, how he knows where to begin. How does a mapmaker learn when a previous mapmaker has made mistakes? That kind of thing. I was startled by this request. My father was, I will always say, a loving man—a good father to me and fun to be with, despite the flaws. But he was a man with a bad habit, an illness, that I did not think would go over well in the classroom.

On the day I said my father would appear, I showed up loaded down with maps and charts, and explained that he was a busy man and, like a traveling salesman, was on the road much of the time. I had enjoyed the research I had done at the public library for this project, and I pinned to the wall an ancient map of California, showing it separated from the landmass, an island floating out to sea. I unrolled another map of people sailing off the edge of the world. I explained to the class how early cartographers made errors based on mistaken impressions of the world. I said that sometimes what we want to believe affects the way we see the world. Who knows, I told them, how our own maps today will be read centuries from now?

The students laughed at my maps, but the teacher was clearly impressed. She wrote a letter to my father. "Ivy is very proud of what you do. She made an excellent presentation today. She made it seem as if being a mapmaker was the most exciting thing in the world. A fine future awaits her, I'm sure." That letter, undelivered, has lain in a box I keep in a drawer. I read it from time to time, for somehow it is the only true reminder of the life I have led.

NINETEEN

THE SUBWAY was packed with morning travelers as I scrambled for a seat on the up-town local. I had left Patricia's early, saying an awkward, unpleasant good-bye. She had asked me not to leave, but I couldn't stay. We both knew it would be some time before we saw one another again. We had tried to apologize, but we had moved into different phases of our lives. There was little left to say.

The subway went two stops before it stalled between stations. An announcement told of signal trouble ahead. The advertisements overhead pre-occupied me as I sat holding Bobby in my lap, the folded stroller in front of me. *Pregnant, embarrassado, habla con nosotros. When I found out I was HIV positive, for me it was the end of the world. Call us when you're tired of living the high life* [a man slouches, needle piercing his arm]. *Do you think you might hurt your child? Call us. Anal warts, fissure, hemorrhoids. Call 1-800 MD-TUSCH.*

The train lurched. A homeless man in a filthy business suit staggered into our car, Styrofoam cup in hand, singing, in a falsetto, "Somewhere over the rainbow, blue birds fly. There's a land that I heard of once in a lullaby." He stumbled toward me—bloodshot eyes, an unbearable stench—and I feared he'd fall on us. I dug into my purse and dropped change into his cup as he shuffled by.

The train stopped again. "Ladies and gentlemen, we regret to inform you . . ." Then all I could hear was static, and a groan went up from the car. "What did he say?" I asked the man beside me. He shrugged. I pulled Bobby closer, wondering where we'd end up that night. I had called Jake to see if we could sleep at his place, but he was on the Island. I called another friend, who offered us their maid's room in the basement of her building.

The conductor came through the car, swearing. Passengers settled in for what would likely be a long delay. With Bobby resting now on my chest (I prayed he would not wake and have to be nursed or changed), I scanned an old copy of *The New York Review of Books.* I started an essay, "Rethinking the Middle East," but found myself quickly distracted, my concentration having been cut to a fraction of what it used to be, and I moved on to a shorter essay on modern American utopian thinkers.

After a paragraph or two I flipped to the personals, where the reading length and required concentration seemed more suited to my frame of mind. *BGM seeks man of similar persuasion for extracurricular whatever. WASP lesbian who won't kiss and tell seeks other women from Greenwich.* There were the usual support groups. *The adult child of adult whatevers. Twelve steps. The head injury support group. Single parents support group.* (Once I had thought of phoning, but realized I had no time to join, and besides, who would watch Bobby?) *Older married man seeks pleasant time with younger woman, no promises but lots of fun.* Then one caught my eye. *Hey, Valentine, are you looking for someone special? I'm handsome, well-built, Brooklyn, SJM in my 30s, seeking ONE cute, slim, Brooklyn nonprofessional SWJF, 27–42, WITHOUT CHILDREN.*

I closed the magazine just as the train started up. At the next station the doors opened and an old woman with long white facial hairs appeared. She stared at me with bewildered eyes and spoke through jagged teeth, eyes bulging; her face would haunt me for a long time. "Is this train going to Coney Island?" she asked. "No, dear," I said, not taking my eyes off her, for fear of what I did not know. "You're going the wrong way." And I pointed as far away from me and Bobby as I could.

I got off the train at Seventy-ninth Street and headed for the Museum of Natural History, where I pushed Bobby past the big boat, an exhibition on explorers, and a series of old exhibits. Life in the Soil, Life on the Farm, Life in the Sea, Life in the Air, Life in the Forest. In Life in the Soil, worms, termites, moles burrowed into the ground. They stared, lifeless and glazed, from their dirt-bound abodes. I headed for the blue whale and sipped a Coke amidst the walruses, the polar bears, animals of the north. Bobby waved an arm at the sharks. The room was dark blue and cold. Children ran everywhere inside this self-contained space. I thought of taking him up to the dinosaurs, but I suddenly felt stifled by all the dead things.

It was midafternoon and I decided to go to a movie. Bobby was asleep, and if he woke, I'd nurse him in the theater. At Loews Eighty-fourth, I had the usual choice of poor films, the kind that Hollywood thinks the American public wants to see. I picked what I thought would be the least offensive and at the same time not be entirely innocuous. It would, of course, have the requisite detective, car chase, and ill-fated romance, but it also promised to deal with one social issue (race relations) and was billed, as if this weren't a contradiction in terms, as a comic thriller.

I bought my ticket and went inside. The ticket taker scrutinized me. "Lady, please fold up your carriage, sit in the back, and if the baby wakes up, you must leave the theater." Once inside, I braced myself for the escalator, then found a seat near the rear, where I sat down, feeling like a derelict, my heart beating. What would I do if my baby woke up? How quickly could I move him to my breast?

Though there were only a few people in the theater—one or two who looked as if they too had no place to go—I found I could not relax. Several fathers with small children who, I assumed, were having their regular Saturday visitation at the movies. How much of a disturbance could I cause? The movie—a psychiatrist's wife is murdered and her husband suspects his lover, who is also a patient, all of which was supposed to be a spoof— brought me only a fleeting pleasure and it was not long before I left that film and snuck into another while the ticket taker was at the popcorn stand. This film appeared to have more drama, but I had missed some key element of the plot—a conversation overheard—which had been covered in the first two minutes. I sat there, intrigued but bewildered, trying to piece together what had happened.

Then Bobby woke and let out a terrible shriek. A hundred heads—this was clearly the more popular movie—turned and stared at me. Half the audience shouted, "Shush!" Though I tried to get him to my breast, he continued to wail. "Take that baby out of here," someone yelled. Embarrassed, I made my way toward the ladies' room. Another movie had just gotten out, and the line to the ladies' room was long. I would, of course, need the handicap stall, but who knew, with this kind of a line, how long it would take me to forge ahead? Bobby, now soaked, was throwing a tantrum. I went to the front of the line.

No one stopped me; no one stood in my way. I changed him and then returned to the first film. I hadn't missed much. Most of the audience was asleep. One man was talking to himself. I put Bobby to my breast and sat back, feeling the soporific effect of his nursing, and watching the movie the way I watch movies on airplanes, without renting the headset, just looking at images for the pleasure of seeing them flicker past me on the screen.

Sitting in the back of the darkened theater I thought how, if my mother were still in my life, I could have dropped off Bobby at her place, seen a movie, had dinner with friends. I wondered what it would be like to have her—telling stories of her past—in my life right now. She would have plastic bags filled with pills. A hacking cough, special diets, creams to keep the wrinkles away. Vitamins to keep her going. She'd come over to watch the baby, hold him up, and say, "I don't think he's getting enough," a subtle disapproval of my nursing. She'd smoke cigarettes and bend over crossword puzzles on her knees, doing them in ink. Maybe she'd regale my dates with stories of her past loves, the ones before my father. The man she sailed off to Catalina with, dolphins leaping around the boat. Her face, once beautiful, now like a prune. Hands crooked. False teeth, hair turned a frizzy gray, body gone to pot. The wizened potentate, her power (the power my remembering has given to her) depleted. It occurs to me as I tell this that my mother, if she is alive, is only in her fifties. Yet I see her as someone very old.

It was dark when the movie let out, and I walked uptown along Broadway, unsure of where I was going. Perhaps, I thought, I was just heading home, returning to a pesticide-poisoned building with a small child. Committing infanticide, suicide. Killing us both. On my way north I was accosted by a man who pulled out a knife. He stood in front of me and told me to give him some money. I stared at him dumbly, for I had never been mugged before. Slowly I reached for my purse, but the man suddenly looked at the baby stroller, then at his knife. He seemed disoriented, as if he were drunk or on drugs. To my surprise, he put the knife away and disappeared down a side street.

Shaken, I continued up Broadway until I came to my block. I pushed the stroller to the front of my building which was dark. Everyone was out. Turning, I looked across the street. A light was on in the apartment of the woman across the way. For a moment I couldn't remember her name. Then it came to me: Mara. She was home. I slipped the stroller down the curb and crossed to the other side.

I pressed the buzzer for a long time before Mara shouted back, "Who is it? Who's there?" I must have leaned too close to the intercom, because I kept shouting, "It's me; it's Ivy." "Who is it?" Mara screamed. "Who's there?"

I pulled my face back. "It's me," I said. "Your neighbor from across the street." She buzzed me in.

Dressed in jeans and an old T-shirt, Mara stared at me as she opened the door. She looked confused. "You said to come over for a drink sometime, so I did. I should have phoned," I told her, "but I didn't have your number."

"Come in," she said, holding the door while I pushed the stroller through. Her apartment was a mess. Toys and paint were everywhere. A box of congealed pizza was on a table. The TV blared with some kids' show. Dishes filled the sink. Clothes lay in clumps, waiting to be washed.

"I'm sorry," I said. "If it's a bad time, I'll leave. I could call you sometime . . ."

Mara began picking up the box of pizza, the dirty clothes. She tossed toys into a basket. Her little boy watched her, then me.

"No," she said. "It's fine. It isn't a bad time."

Suddenly I found myself crumbling; tears came to my eyes. "I didn't know where to go. I can't go home. It's been fumigated. I can't go back to my friend's. Her husband doesn't want children around. They can't have any of their own." She motioned for me to sit down. "You don't even know me. You must think I'm a lunatic. I'm sorry. I'll go." I headed for the door.

She put her hands on her hips, assessing the situation. "No, please stay." She coaxed me to sit down on the sofa. "Now just rest a minute. Alana!" Mara shouted. "Come here, pick up your things. Take Jason and the baby into the other room." Stoically Alana picked up a few things, then took Jason and Bobby into another room.

After they left, I explained everything to Mara more calmly. About having to leave the apartment because of the exterminator and feeling I had no place to go. About not feeling welcome at Patricia's. Wandering the streets of Manhattan. The museum. The movie house. The mugging attempt. That I didn't know where to go.

"And that man you live with?" she asked hesitantly. "I haven't seen you with him in a while."

"We aren't together anymore."

"Oh," she said, "I see." She listened intently to every word I said, staring at me the whole time. When I finished, she put her finger to her chin. She shook her head and sighed. "Would you like some chocolate?" she asked after a long pause.

"Chocolate?"

"Candy," she said.

I thought about this. Chocolate did seem the right thing at the moment. Before I knew what was happening, she had gone to the refrigerator and returned with a box of candy. "My parents sent it to me for Christmas. What am I going to do with a box of chocolates? They always send me the most ridiculous things. I barely eat as it is. So it's been all these months in the refrigerator."

Mara sat on the floor, the box of chocolates open in her lap. "Here, let's eat them."

I slid down off the sofa, and we sat on the floor, stuffing ourselves with caramel creams, marzipan, white chocolate, maple creams, chocolates stuffed with cherries, orange, nougats, coconut, lemon. I sucked on candy that tasted of caramel and chestnut. We were almost through with the box when the children came in—Alana holding Bobby, Jason toddling behind. Alana and Jason reached into the box and scooped up what was left. I put some soft chocolate filling on Bobby's tongue, and he smiled.

"Well," Mara said, "let's see about dinner."

Now we laughed. She ordered a movie. A Western that we could all watch while we ate Chinese food. Though I didn't think I could eat a bite, I found myself ravenous, and we all sat on Mara's bed, eating noodles, watching a grade B Western.

"All right, now, you kids, it's time for bed. Alana, wash up. Brush Jason's teeth. We'll bathe you all in the morning. Ivy, you sleep in my bed; I can sleep on the couch. It's no problem for me."

"Mara, please," I said, "the couch is fine. I don't need your bed."

"Oh, for Pete's sake, take the bed. Get a good night's sleep. You can probably use it."

I nursed Bobby, then put him into the portable crib that Mara set up in the bedroom. In an instant I fell sound asleep. At times I heard the baby cry, but I didn't move. I woke to the sound of boiling water. A light was on in the kitchen. From where I lay, I could see a plume of steam rising from the stove. A pasta pot gurgled as Mara poked at bottles tossing on the surface like rafts in a storm. Bobby was draped over her shoulder. The crib had disappeared from my room.

I tried to get up but found I couldn't move. Instead I stared into the kitchen, into the chiaroscuro, the shadows on the wall. I could paint this portrait, I told myself. Vermeer in a contemporary setting. The smell of fresh linen and warm milk came my way, and I felt like those men in old dramas, infected with jungle fever, who wake to find themselves rescued by a tribe of friendly natives or the local misguided missionaries as they drift between delirium and sleep.

It was late when I got up, almost ten o'clock. The children, even Bobby, were in front of the television, watching cartoons. I went into the living room and found Mara on the floor, eating a bowl of cereal. A large box was on the table. "Here," she said, "this is for you. Open it." Hesitantly I pulled the lid off the box. Inside were clothes—shoes, socks, pants, shirts, T-shirts with alligators on them, little corduroy suits. All labeled 1 TO 2 YEARS. "My mother buys these for him. But Jason's past two now. I thought maybe you could use them."

"Oh, Mara, are you sure? Really, I'll take good care of them."

"Oh, you can have them," she said, putting the lid back on. "I won't be needing them anymore."

TWENTY

THREE DAYS LATER Mara sat in my kitchen, a pot of almond herbal tea between us. In her hands was a pair of scissors, and assorted newspaper ads and D'Agostino's monthly bulletin. She clipped coupons as we talked—for Pampers, Ivory Soap, Kellogg's cereal. On the floor of the living room the children played. "Alana," Mara said, "take the marble out of the baby's mouth." I gasped as a green marble was extracted from Bobby's toothless gums. "Now pick up all the marbles and bring them to me. Now."

She shook her head, reached into her bag, and pulled out a ball—clear plastic with colored objects inside—crayons, paper, books. She tossed them in the direction of Alana. Jason lunged for the ball, and Bobby waved his hands. Mara threw her head back and laughed, and I thought how pretty she was when she was happy. It was the way I'd first seen her across the street when I envied her all that she had. "Jason, don't take that from Bobby." Bobby began to cry as Jason took away the ball, which Alana had given the baby. "Give it back this minute."

She ran her fingers through her long brown hair. "You see, I'm in a very precarious position. If Dave doesn't pay me support, we have no way of living. It's odd, because we have this nice apartment and I make some money as a free-lance writer and I grew up in a nice neighborhood in the suburbs. But I married Dave out of college and I've never really worked. Basically, I'm one support payment away from welfare."

"Wouldn't your parents help you out?"

Mara shrugged and the familiar look of sadness came over her face. "It's a long story. I don't want to be beholden, if you know what I mean."

I nodded. "I guess I know."

"What about you? Do you have family around? Anyone you can turn to?"

"Well, my parents live in Tucson. I work part-time for a jewelry store owner, but he's not someone I can turn to. Still, he helps me out by giving me work."

"No siblings?"

I never knew what to do when someone asked me this. I didn't want to lie. Nor did I want to tell the truth. "No," I said. "I'm an only child."

Mara shook her head. "I had a sister," she said.

"She died. Alana is named after her." She spoke matter-of-factly, but there was something in her voice that told me not to ask any questions about her family, and she wouldn't ask about mine.

"So," Mara said, trying to sound cheerful, "you probably need a baby sitter when you go to work." I had told her that Bobby's father was not helping me out. "Here,"—she scribbled on a piece of paper—"this is a woman I know. She used to baby-sit for a friend of mine. She isn't cheap, but I hear she's very good."

I took the paper and tucked it under a plant that sat on the table. When Mara got up to leave a few moments later, I said, "May I ask you a favor? If it isn't too much . . ."

"Ask," she said.

"I need a few things at the store. Would you mind . . ."

She sat back down. "Take your time," she said. "I'm not in a rush." She picked up her scissors and returned to cutting out coupons. She laid them in front of her in a neat pile, then flipped through them as if they were a deck of cards.

TWENTY-ONE

I AM DREAMING. I know I am dreaming because my mother is in the house. She is cleaning, dusting, baking bread. There are flowers in vases. My mother hums as she goes about her work. She reminds me of Snow White in the house of the dwarfs. These things, of course, never happened. But now I see my mother doing things other mothers do. Leaving cookies on a plate. Sewing name tags in my socks when I go off to camp.

My father comes home from work. He has a job selling furniture or he's a professional man, like a chiropractor. He plops down in front of the news and I climb into his lap. My mother hands him a drink, ruffles his hair. Then Sam and I fight over a doll, a sweater, and I hear my mother's voice: "Now, girls, cut that out. Help me get dinner."

In the middle of the dream I am talking to myself. I say this is not my life. This is my life if my mother had stayed. If she'd been a different mother altogether. We go to a store to buy a dress. We are trying on clothes. She slips easily into a size 8 while I struggle with a 10. We laugh at each other. My mother is slender and dark. Like a flamenco dancer. The saleswoman asks if we are sisters or just friends. We burst out laughing in the dressing room, doubled over.

Then I see myself married, only it is not to Matthew. If my life had been a different life, then the man I would have chosen would not be Matthew. I am pushing a stroller down a wintry residential street in Brooklyn. I have a husband with a briefcase in his hand. We board a plane and fly to Florida. The flight attendant gives a set of wings to Bobby. When we arrive, my parents greet us at the gate. They are healthy, tan. My father, wrinkled but robust, hugs me. My mother is gray, but she reaches out to take Bobby in her arms. She holds him above as if he were a kite she could fly.

In Florida Bobby rides a yellow tricycle. My husband—I call him X in my dream—wears jogging shorts, an orange sweatband. I see him only from the back as he pushes Bobby along. I pick small white flowers. Bobby will grow up to be a lawyer like his father. My parents will die and leave the Florida condo to me and Sam. We will sell it and buy a vacation home together in Maine.

I know I am dreaming, but it is all so clear.

TWENTY-TWO

I BORROWED MONEY from my father—something I'd resisted so far. "I thought you'd never ask," he said. Then I spent days interviewing half the Caribbean—women from Puerto Rico, Belize, Trinidad, and other parts of the third world. Women who were paying other women, perhaps women darker than themselves, to watch their children while they watched mine. There was the nice lady named Luz from Guatemala who had a brain-damaged child back in her country, and she had to send money home; otherwise they would put him in an institution. And there was the woman from Brazil whose child had called 911 because he was cold. (It had taken her two months to get him back from Family Services.) And Marisella, whose brother, a cook, had been laid off. Now he watched her twin girls while she looked for work.

Luz tiptoed around me, whispering whenever she spoke, as if someone were asleep. When she touched the baby, he seemed to be crystal she was struggling not to drop. The woman from Brazil talked all day long, to me, and then to herself as I tried to work. Marisella worked with her Walkman on. Another was watching soap operas when I returned from the store. I was at the point of despair when I remembered that Mara had given me the phone number of a woman she knew. I found it still tucked under the plant where I'd put it the day Mara came over.

The next day Viviana walked in. She wore a floral skirt and a neat white blouse, carried a dainty purse, and complained about her aching back and the thugs on the subways. She was a compact Jamaican woman whose hair was tinted pale green, and she had blue eyebrows to match. She looked at me and said, "You're pale. You need to get out more." She glanced around the apartment. "And I can only work nights."

"Nights?"

"That's right. My husband, he works days. I work nights. Keeps the marriage going," she said with a cackle. "I can arrange to work days, but it will take some doing. For the moment I can work twelve hours, six to six if you want, but it's not cheap and I never work weekends."

"I suppose nights would be all right for now . . ."

"Maybe I could change to days down the road, but I've got to fix it with my husband. Because of the kids."

"How many kids do you have?" I asked.

"A few more than you've got."

I nodded, feeling uncomfortable about hiring someone in the first place. "I can't pay more than two hundred a week," I said, hoping she'd leave. "Maybe two-fifty," which was my week's income if I worked full time for Mike—if he had the work for me.

"I'm used to getting three hundred, sometimes more." She frowned. "Who recommended me to you anyway?"

"Mara Lange. She lives across the street. She's a friend of . . ."

"I know her." Viviana was walking away. "Let's see the baby." She looked around the apartment, at the four crammed rooms, the studio by the window.

"I'm not married," I told her.

"Doesn't bother me." She shrugged.

"About the money . . ."

"Don't worry about the money now. Where's the baby? Are you hiding him?"

I pointed to the bedroom, where Bobby was lying in his crib. She touched his cheek. "Oh, he's a cute little fella." She cackled again as she picked him up. I expected Bobby to squirm, but he didn't.

She touched his cheek. "He's got a rash. No big deal. Got some A and D ointment?"

"A and D ointment?"

"Just get some. Oh, he's very cute. Nice. You and me, we're going to get on just fine." She tickled him until he laughed. Then she began taking his clothes out of the drawers of the changing table. "He can't wear this anymore." She held up a pair of small pajamas. "And he can't wear this." She rummaged through the other drawers. "I've got references if you want them."

"No," I said, "that's all right," thinking she wouldn't be with me long. Besides, Mara had recommended her.

She looked at me, shaking her head. "It's up to you."

"I'll look for someone who can work days, but nights are fine for now." Though the arrangement seemed a bit bizarre, I was used to working in the evening and at night. I could get a lot of work done then and sleep in the early hours while Viviana watched Bobby.

"Whatever you want is fine with me." Then, looking into the mirror, she apologized because her hair was turning green. "I told that woman not to use that strong rinse on me." She said nothing about her blue eyebrows, though later when I commented she said, "Blue? Am I using blue?"

The first night, Viviana sat in the living room,

watching me paint. "I don't feel comfortable," I told her, "with you sitting there across from me."

"So I'll go into the bedroom, but you got the baby sleeping in here and I'm supposed to watch the baby, right?"

"Maybe you could just come when he cries."

Viviana snorted, put her hands on the portable crib, and pushed Bobby into the bedroom. "I'll move him out later. Poor child."

"I've never done this before," I said. "Hired someone to work for me. I don't feel very good about it, I suppose."

"Look, you've got to work and I've got to work, so what difference does it make if I work for you?"

I had seen the baby sitters lined up in front of schools or on park benches—the blacks, the Hispanics, the European au pairs. I had watched them chattering among themselves with varying degrees of attention and caring toward the children. Some were loving; others seemed indifferent. I had a friend whose daughter spoke with a slight West Indian accent, the result of spending more time with her nanny than with her parents. Once I saw a nanny slap a child in a sandbox and I wondered what would happen if the mother knew.

But most of the nannies with whom white New York women involved themselves in this neocolonial relationship simply had their own children to support. I'd read that the infants of wet nurses often starved to death in England, because their mothers gave all their milk to the children of the rich.

On a trip out west with Matthew we observed a herd of buffalo grazing. Apart from the herd, off to the side, was a small contingent of sleeping baby buffalos and two or three grownups—what appeared to be an aged female and two pregnant females—watching over them during their nap. A day care center, it looked like. Even animals must find the way to watch over their young. I read an interview once with the wife of a Mormon polygamist; she said that polygamy was the perfect arrangement for a working mother because there were so many potential caretakers.

So I too found myself forced into this symbiosis. I hired Viviana because I liked her and it seemed clear that she would do her job, albeit at night, and not mince any words. That evening I nursed Bobby and went to my work table while Viviana sat in the light of the bedroom, her green hair shimmering like the harvest moon.

Despite my desire to be up by seven, I woke at almost nine o'clock to the smell of coffee brewing. I wandered through the tiny rooms of my apartment and saw that all of Bobby's clothes had been washed and were hanging up to dry. Bobby was asleep, swaddled and clean in his crib, and Viviana was putting on her coat to leave.

"You did all that wash while I slept?"

"That and more," she said. "He should sleep for at least two hours. See you tonight."

She came each night, and when I woke in the morning the chores were done, the house spotless, Bobby was clean, and I could work for a few hours before he rose from his morning nap. She would wake him at about six and keep him up for a few hours until he got his bottle and morning nap. I was able to work until midmorning. I began to feel like a person again. "Viviana," I said to her one night, "I don't know how long I can afford to keep you."

"Doesn't matter. Keep me as long as you can," she said, pulling at a strand in the mirror. "God, my hair sure is green."

One morning I woke to a pouring rain. A deluge of biblical proportions. I crawled out of bed and saw Viviana holding Bobby up to the window. "Look at that rain, young man," Viviana said to my four-month-old son in her hands. "You'd better cancel all your appointments."

"Viviana," I said, sitting on the arm of a chair in my nightgown, "can we talk?"

"Sure, we can talk. What do you want to talk about?"

"I want to talk about days. I'd like you to work for me days."

She shrugged. "I don't know. Arnold won't like it."

"Look, I need to go back to work. I can get a full-time job and I'll be able to pay you a little more. I want you to stay with us."

"I'll think about it," she said.

The following week Viviana began work at nine in the morning. I called Mike and said I needed a full-time job. "I have a baby sitter, so I can put in more hours. I need to make some money."

That morning I got up early and showered. When Viviana arrived, I was supposed to head out the door. Instead, I found myself straightening up, sorting through papers. I kissed my son, hugged him, played with him until Viviana said, "Why don't you go to work?"

"Will you be all right? Look, here's the number. Call me if there's anything at all. Do you think he'll be all right? Do you have enough milk?"

Viviana looked at me harshly and said, "One of us is walking out that door, and it's either you or me, so you decide."

I left with a sense that I'd forgotten something I needed to do. But what it was eluded me. Emergency numbers were taped to the wall; the bottles were all prepared. Viviana had keys and knew where to reach me. Yet as I walked toward the subway I wondered whether I had interviewed Viviana enough. I had, after all, never before left her alone with Bobby. I had hardly left anyone alone with him. What would happen to Bobby while I was gone? I had left him with someone I hardly knew. A person who came into my life and began to care for my child. But what did I know about her, really?

I arrived at Mike's, said hello to Alma and Suzette. "So how's the little man?" Alma said.

"Oh, fine, fine." I sat down to work—a pin that needed to be reset. But it was an ugly, foolish piece and I couldn't imagine who would wear such a thing. Someone who had to have things they didn't really want or need. The pin would probably just go back into the jewelry box, never to be worn again. As I worked, my mind wandered. Did Viviana look both ways before crossing the street? Would she go down the wrong street and get caught in crossfire? Perhaps I should have checked her out further. Blood test. Police record. She could just walk out the door and disappear. I had no home address for her. I had no way of finding her.

I picked up the phone and dialed but there was no answer. I waited a few moments and tried again. Then I phoned Mara, thinking I could ask her more about Viviana, but she wasn't home. Mike came into the workroom and saw me on the phone. "Ivy," he said, "it's a beautiful day. They've gone for a walk. Anybody in her right mind would."

"Of course," I said, knowing he was right. Smiling, I settled back to work. The pin was a circle of diamonds and sapphires with a ruby center. Past its prime, if it ever had a prime. I envisioned it worn by someone's great-grandmother, a frigid, meddling woman who damaged all who came within her grasp.

Picking at the setting, I contemplated the properties of stones. Diamonds and sapphires, purple onyx and mother-of-pearl. The ancients believed that some could cast a spell and others, like crystal, could heal. Ruby cured inflammation and flatulence; yellow sapphire was an antidote to poison. For Emerson the ruby was a drop of frozen wine. The Holy Grail was carved from emerald. Emeralds predict the future; diamonds protect against evil. It's not for nothing that they're a girl's best friend.

What you look for in a diamond is clarity. The hardest mineral of all, unlike gold, which is the most pliable yet the strongest. Only a diamond can cut itself. So how did the first carver cut the first diamond, I wondered. In the refractions of diamonds I've seen the faces of the miners who pull them from the earth. I cannot work with these stones and not think of the men's toil. In books I've seen the dark, despairing faces of the men of South Africa, men who often die—if not in the mines then in riots outside the mines. They riot because the conditions they live in are horrible and because they are separated from family and home. When they go to see their children, they are docked their pay. I wish I had another way of earning a living.

I went to the phone again, but there was still no answer. Even though it was a beautiful spring day, shouldn't they be home by now, getting ready for a nap or a bath? Where could they have gone for so long? I wish I had checked her references. She'd offered them to me, but I had refused. I'd just believed what she told me. But I didn't know her at all; she was a complete stranger. I had entrusted my flesh and blood to a stranger. I told Mike I had to go. I had an emergency. I had been there only three hours, but already I was out the door.

I raced home and walked into an empty apartment. It was neat, the dishes put away. Everything smelled fresh and clean; the bed was made, the laundry done. But there was no sign of them. I have been here before, I told myself. This isn't the first time I've come home and found everything gone. I rushed back into the street and walked up and down the block, wondering whom I could turn to, whom I could call. Mara had recommended Viviana, but, then, how well did I know Mara? And how well had she known Viviana? I walked across the street and buzzed Mara, but she still wasn't home. I headed over to Riverside Park, where I could clear my head and think. I'd figure out what to do.

In the park the dogwood was in bloom. Pink-and-white blossoms fluttered down. First I walked north, toward 116th Street. The park was full of joggers, prams, dog walkers. But Viviana and Bobby were nowhere to be seen. When I got farther north than I thought they'd be, I turned south. I passed the same joggers, the same prams, the same dog walkers. Still no sign of them. How far could she have gone? I began to think about how I'd track Viviana down. Mara would give me the name of the friend for whom Viviana had worked, and she'd know how to locate her. Eventually I would find them.

I was approaching Ninety-sixth Street when I saw a bench lined with nannies. There sat Viviana in the shade with Bobby. He had balloons tied to his stroller and was laughing. Viviana was singing to him. She looked up and saw me standing there. "What are you doing here? Why aren't you at work?"

"I called. There was no answer. I got worried. I came home."

"Good, now go back to work." She spoke with annoyance. "Haven't you got better things to do?"

TWENTY-THREE

M Y MOTHER took a job at the At First Sight marriage chapel. It wasn't on the Strip, where the rows of marriage chapels were like the Hitching Post and Cupid's Arrow. The At First Sight was located a little way outside of town, along the desert road coming into Vegas on a dry dusty lot surrounded by scrub cactus and piñon. It took me a while to understand that the name didn't have anything to do with the fact that the chapel was one of the first things you saw when you entered the Valley of Fire.

My mother got mostly the in-transit trade. The ones who on impulse zipped off the highway, got married, gambled away what they had in their pockets, and hopped back into the car. Nine out of ten times, she said, they were heading west. Not many people heading back east stopped to get married. People heading east, my mother said, had no more illusions.

Business was very good when she went to work there because of the nuclear tests at Yucca Flats. Often the tests were delayed due to weather, and the soldiers, dying of boredom, came into Vegas, met some girls at the casinos, and got married, just like that. At times I suspected that my mother herself left town with one of these men.

Getting married on the Strip was more exciting than painting rocks—an assignment one of their commanding officers had conceived for them, one of the soldiers told my mother on a day when I was there, helping her fold bows. The officer had them paint the rocks brilliant shades of glacier blue, autumn bronze, and harvest gold. Make the desert beautiful, he said. One of the soldiers complained to my mother that Korea had been more interesting than this.

But the nuclear tests were good for business. The town went all out. There were atomic hairdos (beehives for women), atomic burgers served with lots of mushrooms, mushroom cakes, swimming pools filled with mushrooms. Miss Atomic Blast was crowned. Couples liked to be married during the blasts. They liked the light. They'd stand outside and at the exact moment of the explosion, the minister declared them man and wife. I assisted at such weddings. We watched the great glare go up in the sky and I'd be momentarily blinded. Then my mother would nudge me to toss the rice.

My mother was a dour woman when she went

to work at the marriage chapel, bitter with her lot. She might have done better directing a funeral home. But she liked her job. It gave her something to do. She talked to me about the couples who came to her. She had a lot of responsibility there. She made the arrangements for the flowers, procured licenses, and even helped trembling lovers who were running away, or who had met only the night before, write their own service.

On days off from school or on weekends, she made me come with her. She worked the midday shift, and I hated to go because it meant I couldn't go with my father when he drove for Lucky Cab. I sat all day long in this dry patch at the edge of the desert and watched couples come and go. She assigned me tasks. I folded colored ribbons for the bouquets and lined them up on a rack like a rainbow; I made sure that the green Tupperware pitcher that read RICE wasn't empty; I dusted and vacuumed, though this was pointless in such an arid place. Then we'd sit and wait for a couple to show up.

Sometimes two drunk people who'd been gambling staggered in and, even though we knew they'd probably just met, my mother made the arrangements. I used to wonder—as she showed couples floral displays or musical arrangements—why they didn't run screaming into the desert. But they always seemed relieved inside the cool chapel with the soft yellow walls, and for a few moments they were at peace while the minister, the Reverend Remlow Blevins, performed the ceremony. Sometimes Indians stopped. We had a special outdoor chapel for them, complete with a painting of the sky and a wooden eagle with chipped beak and broken wing. At other times a couple clutching a small baby would come in, looking weary and blank. And when the ceremony was done, I'd toss rice and shout congratulations as the dumbstruck pair got back in their car and headed west at breakneck speed.

I would watch as the Reverend Remlow Blevins married people in his perfunctory, dispassionate way, and I thought to myself even then that he knew something about life that I didn't know. He knew how it could lead you astray, how a mistake could throw you off for a lifetime. He was a pasty-faced man with slicked-back hair and dead gray eyes, and it was hard to believe that he lived in this heat; his complexion was more like that of a shut-in than a man who baked in a marriage chapel in the middle of the Mojave. I wondered why he didn't terrify his clients, as he liked to call them, with those dead eyes.

The worst time for me was those days when the dust blew or when a winter's freeze set in and customers were few. On those dreary days, when all I wanted was to be moving through the dark, timeless, womblike space of the casino, dropping slugs into one-armed bandits or watching my father's smooth movements with the cards, I'd have to sit with my mother, stringing bows for bouquets, with Remlow Blevins staring out at U.S. 91, searching for trembling couples who wanted to be married.

My mother sat with her thick black hair, putting rice into the Tupperware pitcher or wrapping ribbons around the stems of the bouquets, cursing my father for the life she led. She cursed him for having swept her away, though it seemed to be the one fond memory of him she had—the way he married her. Perhaps it was this memory that led her to work in a marriage chapel in Vegas. I knew my parents almost as long as they'd known each other. That is, she accepted his breathless proposal in a hot-air balloon three weeks after they met, and they were married a few weeks later. I was born nine months from the date of their marriage. Their love affair, from all I can gather, was an impassioned fling that managed to extend itself through eight years and the birth of two children before my mother took off.

The hot-air balloon belonged to a friend of my father's. My father was a handsome, compact man with a powerful way about him, but my mother, though not exactly virtuous, came from old religious stock and would not easily give in. The balloon he borrowed that day was yellow and red and green; the colors, when my mother spoke of them, made me think of the confetti of the losers' tickets from the track that my father threw in my hair.

It was a clear Saturday afternoon in the Los Angeles basin in the mid-fifties when my parents stepped into the small basket under the giant balloon and my mother looked up at all those colors set against the sky. My father's friend released the sand bags before my mother could protest, and they sailed away. She told me how smooth the lift-off was, how effortless the balloon's steady rise; she said she thought that life could be like this and they'd just go up and up forever.

Then the balloon sailed over what had once been an unsettled land of relentless sun and barren earth, a land of boiling tar pits and hellish marshes, filled with animal remains. They sailed west, out to sea, toward Catalina, and then the winds brought them back, carrying them along the edge of the land and up the coast along the Palisades and out across to the Hollywood sign. They skirted the desert where purple flowers bloomed, and skimmed above Wilshire Boulevard, looking down on mansions with swimming pools, ensconced in cooling palms. They sailed the emerald cliffs of Malibu and above a turquoise sea until, when my father asked if she'd marry him, there was nothing my mother could say but yes.

TWENTY-FOUR

A T SEVEN O'CLOCK on a warm summer's night I rang Mara's bell. She opened the door, dressed in a short black cocktail dress, black stockings, and heels. She had her hair down but pulled softly off her face with gold clips on either side. I wore a black skirt and a white blouse, but Mara was much more dressed up than I. "I don't think I can go out with you," I said.

She looked me up and down. "You look fine." I pushed Bobby's stroller in and Alana and Jason raced to take him. We had hired Viviana for the evening to baby-sit for all three children at Mara's. She was already there, getting the children's dinner ready. Mara leaned over and whispered to me, "Her hair is green."

"I know," I told her. "It's all right. I think I should go put on a dress." It was months since I'd gotten dressed up. Mara had phoned a few nights before to say she'd been invited to a party for a friend of hers—a TV producer—who was giving a dancing party at some celebrity's loft. A good band, Dead in the Water, was playing, and Mara had asked if I'd be her date.

"It's going to be pitch black in there, with loud music. No one's going to care what you're wearing. And besides," she said, looking me up and down once again, "you look fine."

I went into the kitchen with Bobby, and Viviana whistled. "Don't you look nice, um-huh. You might not be coming home tonight."

"I'll be home."

"Stay out late. I don't want to see you before midnight."

"What time do you want us home?"

"You put me in a cab, I don't care if it's daybreak. Just don't come knocking on this door early, because I won't open it."

Mara looped her arm through mine. "Let's go."

"Everything'll be all right?" I asked Viviana.

"Not if you don't leave," she replied.

"It'll be all right. It will be fine." Mara smiled, tossing her head back the way she did when she felt at ease. "We're going to have fun."

Half an hour later we walked into a loft building in Tribeca. The building on the outside was dingy, and we took the service elevator, with dozens of other people, to the twelfth floor. The door opened onto a huge open space, dark except for a strobe light, hard rock blaring. "Act as if you know someone," Mara said, squeezing my hand. "Be brave."

I took a deep breath and followed her into the room. My breasts were heavy, my body round, and I felt like a wallflower being introduced by an insistent relative. "Whose place is this?"

"I'm not sure," Mara said. "I don't even see my friend here."

"Oh, great."

"Just try to have a good time, Ivy. You owe it to yourself. It will make you a better person."

The room was filled with people in black T-shirts and black stretch pants or short skirts, and Mara was right: no one cared what anyone else was wearing, or what anyone else looked like, for that matter. The air was permeated with the smell of body sweat and sour wine and the pungent scent of cheese puffs and stuffed mushroom caps. "I'm getting old," I said.

"No, you aren't. That man over there is going to ask you to dance." We were leaning against a railing, drinks in hand, and I glanced in the direction she was pointing. An attractive man with a mustache was looking our way. "No, you're his type," I said.

"Oh, Ivy, you don't know your own power."

"I'm just going to call Viviana," I said, feeling suddenly unsure. "I want to be sure everything is all right."

"It's all right," Mara said, catching me by the arm. But I pulled away.

"I'll be right back," I said, waving. I walked down a hallway in search of a phone and finally came on one in a room full of jackets. A woman in black tights and a black halter top with six rings on each earlobe was talking; it appeared from her hunched-over posture that she'd be on for a while. Besides, I knew Viviana would only scold me for calling, so I decided to go back and find Mara.

I must have left the room by a different door, because I found myself wandering down a long, narrow corridor; it was dark and smoky, filled with people drinking, kissing, and I was lost among them. I turned up a vestibule that opened on to another end of the loft, into a large room with a fireplace and a mirror.

Dancing couples, dressed almost exclusively in black, cast looming shadows on the wall. They all looked like the woman who'd been on the phone, except that the flashing strobe made them seem to be writhing, as if they were in pain or burning in hell. I searched for Mara, but couldn't find her. Feeling unsteady and uncertain in the crowd, I thought I'd check my appearance in the wide mirror on the wall. I moved closer to see if my hair was in place, if I needed to put lipstick on, but when I was actually standing in front of it, I did not see my reflection at all. Instead, I stared at the room, the gas fire in the fireplace, the black dancing figures. But I wasn't there, and the space where I stood was blank.

Then I saw Mara, waving at me from what appeared to be the reflection in the mirror—the place where I was not. It took me a moment to realize that I was not looking into a mirror, but rather into a large window set in a wall that connected two identical rooms. The fake gas fires, the stark black furniture, even the dancing figures dressed in black, were all the same. Mara beckoned to me from where my own image should have been, and I made my way around the wall to join her.

"I thought I'd never see you again," she said.

"Me too," I told her.

She was standing beside a man who was well dressed, a bit too well dressed, in a padded almost Armani jacket and beige chinos, a dark gray shirt and cranberry tie. He introduced himself as a psychologist of loss, "one who specializes," Mara informed me, "in the physiology of the body's responses to a loss. The loss of body parts," she said.

"Oh, nice." I smiled. He smiled back.

"You know, how you feel after an appendectomy, a mastectomy. Cosmetic surgery. There's more postoperative depression with cosmetic surgery than with any other kind."

"Interesting," I said. I tried to keep smiling. He and Mara were obviously in the middle of a conversation; he resumed talking about the rush of blood to the limbs, the release of the bowels. Under extreme physical distress, I heard him say, the colon will dry up, causing decay.

Mara winked at me and I excused myself. At the long Formica bar I ordered a vodka. The man with the mustache who Mara said had been looking at me was doing so again. He came over until his body almost rested against mine. "Would you like to dance?" he asked with a foreign accent.

"No." I smiled. "I have to call my baby sitter."

He thought about this for a moment. "Are you married?"

"No."

He smiled. "Well, when you come back, would you like to dance?"

Thinking about the woman in black who was probably still on the phone, I told him we could dance now. He said his name was Hans and he worked in production design for a small independent film studio. He was from somewhere in Scandinavia and we danced for a long time, first to disco music and then to some slow numbers when it got late, and he pulled me to him. Mara disappeared again in the crowd as we sailed away, though I saw her waving from time to time. He was drunk and so was I and I didn't care when he pressed his body against mine. It had been so long since I'd felt a man's body, since I had felt desire rising within me.

He held me in the dimly lit room and his breath

was warm against my throat. Again I let him press himself against me, and I knew that I would go on. That other things would happen in my life. "I'll call you," he said when it was time to go. "Give me your number." I wrote it on a slip of paper I had in my purse and gave it to him. I never heard from him again.

It was midnight when we staggered out, my head spinning, my body still warm from being held. Mara looped her arm through mine, and I wasn't ready to go home. "I'm hungry," I said. "Let's get something to eat."

Mara nodded. "God, I'm hungry too. I'm famished."

"I'm drunk," I said.

"I am too."

"We'll pay for this tomorrow, won't we?"

"Yes, we will."

A diner was open across the street. It had bright pink and blue neon in the window and small cacti on the sill. We made our way to a red booth where the vinyl screeched as we slid inside. We both ordered cheeseburgers with the works, French fries, cole slaw, and Diet Cokes. "I could eat a horse," she said.

"So could I."

"It's good to get out. You know, I hardly ever do it. Not since Dave and I split. Before, when we were together, well, we went out a lot. Especially when Dave got nominated for his Emmys."

"I know. You wore that blue sequined gown. The strapless one. And you put your hair high on your head."

She looked at me oddly, then laughed. "That's right. I don't think I could get into that dress anymore." Then she cocked her head. "You *have* been spying on me."

"Well, not exactly spying. I just watched you. When I did my work. I saw you with manuscripts under your arm. I imagined you were publishing romance novels under a pseudonym."

Mara got a distant look. "Yes," she said, "that would be nice. I wrote a few scripts, actually, for television, but nothing much happened. Now I just do health and fitness articles, not that I know a thing about health or fitness. Not what you imagined, is it?"

"Not exactly."

"So have I surprised you? Or disappointed you?"

I thought about this for a few moments. "Yes, I suppose you have. Surprised me, that is. You aren't quite what I imagined."

"And what was that?"

"Someone tougher, less vulnerable. Stronger, I suppose. You're really a nice person. But that's not how you look. That day when I just arrived at your house, I thought you'd throw me out. Most sane people would have, but you were very nice. I must have been out of my mind, but you were kind to me. It wasn't what I would have expected from watching you. I'll never forget that."

"Something must have let you think you could come to me."

"I don't know. You seemed so . . ." I searched for the word. "Hardened."

"Oh, you saw my carapace. Isn't that the word —the shell of a crustacean? I learned that in biology, my first year in high school."

"That was the year you grew your carapace?" I asked. I ate my cheeseburger slowly, my eyes fixed on her.

"It was the year my sister died." She said it carefully, deliberately. "We were studying crustaceans in biology. Lobsters, crabs, that kind of thing. I thought I wanted to be a doctor. In fact, I did want to be a doctor, so I took this elective biology course. Advanced Placement. Then Alana got sick. She was well one day, and the next day she was sick. We were just two years apart. She was very pretty. She had long hair like honey and she sang folk songs like Joan Baez, Sixties' stuff. Anyway, she was my best friend. She was fine, happy, healthy. One day she didn't feel well, and six weeks later, she was dead. Pancreatic cancer. Just like that. You're fine, then you're gone."

"It sounds awful," I murmured, "to lose your sister like that."

Mara shook her head. "It wasn't just that I lost my sister," she went on. "That was bad enough. I lost my whole family, really. They just fell apart. Don't talk to me about families," she said. "Nobody's had one quite like mine." I thought of saying something—of telling her the truth about my own—but Mara looked so brittle that I wondered how it was that I'd ever imagined she was strong. It was the toughness I saw in her face, but that was something learned. An acquired skill. I should have known it all along.

"My father used to go to flea markets every Saturday. He loved to take us with him," she went on. "He brought home all kinds of junk. Mugs with porcelain frogs in them, old bottles, tattered lace doilies. Once he brought home the burning bush from a rummage sale. It sat in our living room for ages. He was a kind, fun-loving guy and then Alana died and it all stopped. We had this umbrella in the backyard on the patio and my parents sat under the umbrella the whole spring and summer into the fall. They stayed until the leaves fell on the umbrella. They didn't do anything. My father never went to work. There were no meals. I don't know what he did about his job. They just sat. I tried to do things to make them happy. I cooked them special meals. One day I made a picnic, but they wouldn't go anywhere, so I put the food on the patio table under the umbrella and they picked at it, but they wouldn't eat it. Nothing helped. It didn't matter that I was alive. That I was fifteen. Nobody noticed. Nobody cared. I even went through a wild period—drugs, sex, you name it. My grades fell. My parents gave me these halfhearted reprimands, but they weren't my parents anymore. Did you ever see that science fiction movie about the giant pods that take people over . . ."

"Invasion of the Body Snatchers," I said.

"Well, it was as if they'd been snatched."

"I can't really imagine what that would be like . . ."

"No, I guess not. You've never had a sibling. You've got your family in Tucson. I guess it's pretty difficult to imagine."

I wanted to tell Mara then about living in an abandoned Dairy Queen and pretending that my father was a cartographer, about my mother and Sam leaving when I was seven years old, but I had lied to her and told her I didn't have a sister and that my parents lived in Tucson. I was afraid that she wouldn't like me if I suddenly blurted out the truth. Or if she learned I'd lied. So I just said, "But I've had a child and his father doesn't want to be married to me. I can imagine loss."

"Yes, I suppose you can."

"I don't think I'll see him again, not if I can help it." I laughed nervously. "There's no point. But it hasn't been easy . . ."

"No, I imagine it hasn't. With Dave it was easier because I was ready. It wasn't that he was seeing other women or didn't have much time for the children; somehow I was able to ignore those things. It was when he began to sit around that I couldn't stand him anymore. When he was waiting for work or when something went wrong, and he just sat. I said to him, 'I've seen enough of that. I've lived with that before.' "

I grinned. "Well, you are tough the way I thought."

"I used to see you at the window," Mara said. "I used to wonder what's a nice girl like that doing with that egotistical guy."

"You watched me too?"

"Not exactly." She cocked her head. "Not consciously. There was something about him—don't ask me what. Not that I spent much time looking at you. I really didn't, but I'd see you in the window and you looked kind of dreamy. And he seemed so sure of himself. I don't think he was right for you."

I smiled. "Well, I'm glad to hear that. I don't think so either. But it's nice to hear it from someone else."

"I'm glad you said hello to me that day."

"I'm glad I did too."

We paid our bill and walked outside. Mara took my hand as we crossed the street to hail a taxi. Two men whistled at us, thinking we were gay. Mara gave them the finger, tossed her head back, and laughed. The night had a remarkable clarity, unusual for New York at any time of the year. The sky was cloudless and you could almost see stars, or the promise of stars. There was a half moon. I looked up and took a deep breath. "It's a beautiful night," I said.

She hailed a cab and we tumbled in. "I don't want to go home," I said.

"I don't especially either. Let's go to the Statue of Liberty. Let's ride a buggy around Central Park."

"We'd better go," I said, reluctantly. "We'll do this again."

She closed her eyes once the cab started; it was cozy and warm. A bulletproof shield protected the driver from us or us from the driver as the case may be and we rode in silence. Mara's head rested against my shoulder, and I ached to tell her who I really was, about my mother and Sam and what my life had been, but perhaps she would never forgive me for my lie.

I let my head rest against hers as we raced up Eighth Avenue, through Times Square, past Lincoln Center. The streets were empty for Manhattan, and we made all the green lights, heading uptown.

TWENTY-FIVE

THREATS. They are everywhere. I stopped slipping ice cubes into Bobby's mouth after Mara told me not to. ("But they melt," I'd protested. "Not before you're dead," she replied.) She instructed me how to cut hot dogs, which Bobby would be eating in a few months. In half lengthwise, then in smaller pieces. The number one cause of accidental death in children between the ages of one and two is from hot dogs. Lethal. Everything around me has become a danger. Nothing is immune. The obvious ones—fish bones, muggers, Alar—are not of much concern. Now it is electric outlets, cotton balls, mobiles over cribs. A million ways to choke or suffocate present themselves, things I'd never contemplated before.

The night before Bobby was born I had taken a baby safety class. I sat, huge, already in labor, though I didn't know it at the time, amidst terrified couples holding hands. "What do you do if your child is plugged into an electric outlet?" Mrs. Volkan had droned on in her Austrian accent. "What do you do if your baby is on fire?" For the latter you throw a blanket over him and beat down the flames. For the former, get a broom and sweep him away.

Even though Bobby has a few months before he begins to crawl, I baby-proof everything. Plastic plugs into sockets, latches on doors. I move the Drāno (I've heard terrible stories) and the Ajax to the top shelf. People—perfect strangers—regale me with stories of what happens if you drink Joy. I look at the boxes of jewels I keep around the house for repair. The worst-case scenarios present themselves. Bobby pulling himself up to swallow a diamond. A gold band. I move these to top drawers. I study the apartment. Corners of tables become enemies. I tape them smooth. I hide the plastic bags. The bars of the crib can choke. A mobile, the kind with plastic animals that go around, can kill. There are a million stories of the horrible deaths of children, not from violence, but from the basic tools of living. The world is full of weapons. We all suddenly are under siege.

And this is only what happens at home. It says nothing of the world outside, where random violence, disease, the fortuitous abound. An unemployed actor, walking by a building under construction, is struck dead by a steel beam. A child asleep in his bed in the projects is shot by a stray bullet. Pictures of missing children take on new meaning. These are not the faces of the abused, the neglected, the ignored. This is a child who was taken to a circus or went camping with his dad, never to be seen again.

In the supermarket one day I leave Bobby in the carriage with the checkout girl. I know her well and I am too tired to carry the baby as I shop. When I return, the manager scolds me. "If her back was turned, you know how easy it would be for someone to walk out of here with that kid?" Though I resist them, I read the stories of the things that can happen. A wind blows in the window of a cafeteria where children eat sandwiches and sip chocolate milk; a dozen of them are crushed. A man puts his pregnant lover on a plane from England, and everyone, including many college students returning home for Christmas, are blown away. One mother writes to the *New York Times* that her life is over. A father holds a hospital staff at bay with a gun while he pulls the plug on his fifteen-month-old son who has lived as a vegetable since swallowing a balloon. A balloon.

Anything becomes possible. The world is a threat. The ingredients on packages. (What is sodium chloride? What is BHT?) What are the additives? What do they spray the plants with? Will my son have bone cancer in two decades because of what I'm feeding him now? Will he get on the wrong plane? Stories that were other people's problems now become mine. I weep as I read of a school bus that bursts into flames. And then there are drugs. And of course war. He could be drafted. I find myself praying as I never have for peace.

There are other cities, countries, where we could live. But Los Angeles had 137 days of ozone alert last year, and it has over two thousand gangs. DC has the most murders, but New York has more random crimes. There are street children in Seattle, ghetto crimes in Chicago. San Francisco seemed a nice place to live until the expressway collapsed.

I ponder how to protect this child. What can I do to keep him safe? I find myself, night after night, weighing the odds.

TWENTY-SIX

ONE SATURDAY afternoon in May, Mara took all the kids to the park so that I could stay home and paint. She had taken Bobby and Jason in a double stroller with Alana walking beside. I was to meet them for dinner. I sat at my work table, the sun streaming in. The sun felt good on my face and I was happy to have the time to myself. I was working on a photorealist desertscape—an empty road leading to a vanishing point. But set against the mountains, coming naturally out of their shapes, was the face. In the strong light the face looked clearer than it had in the past, and I felt myself on the brink of discovery. It was at the moment when everything seemed to come together that Matthew phoned. But I was not surprised. He seemed to have a sixth sense about me. He must have felt me slipping away.

The machine was on and I let it answer. When

I heard his voice, I did not move. His message was simple. He wanted to see his son. "Ivy," I heard him say, "it's me, Matt. I know it's been awhile; I hope it's long enough now. Maybe you're home screening your calls, but whenever you listen to this, I just want to tell you that I've been thinking and I miss you and Bobby a great deal. I know this may sound strange, but Bobby's been on my mind lately. I feel that he should know me in some capacity. I am, after all, his father, whether I wanted this or not; it seems to me that I ought to have some kind of relationship with him."

It wasn't that I hadn't thought about Matthew, though it was weeks since we'd spoken. More and more as I held Bobby, I could see Matthew's eyes, his hair. When I looked at Bobby naked, I saw Matthew's long waist, his foreshortened limbs. More and more Bobby's features defined themselves by his father's. And beyond this, in my own body a longing had set in. At night my body trembled with desire and I wanted what I had not had in so long. If I closed my eyes, I could almost feel Matthew's hands as they traveled down my back. But just as I had begun to put him in the same place where, I suppose, I had long ago tucked my mother and Sam, Matthew was calling.

He talked to the machine for a while, and I still did not answer the phone. It was odd, because at that moment, listening to Matthew's disembodied voice, I wanted him more than I ever had. I wanted to feel his hands on my body, his mouth against my mouth. I wanted him in a way that was strange and desperate. When he stopped talking and the machine clicked off, I resolved not to phone him back.

But a week later he phoned again, and my machine wasn't on. When I picked up the receiver, he said, "Ivy, it's me. I want to talk to you."

"Please," I said, "please leave us alone."

"Look, I miss you. I want to see you and I want to see the baby."

"You should have thought of that months ago," I told him. "You've had plenty of time to think about that."

"Will you meet me? Please? I just want to talk. Couldn't we just meet and discuss this?"

We agreed to go two nights later to an Italian restaurant on the West Side, a place we used to drop in for a bottle of Chianti and pasta. Viviana had agreed to stay late and watch Bobby. I told her I needed to speak with his father and I wanted to do so alone. But I was looking forward to the occasion. I thought about what I would wear, how I wanted to look. I put on a gray jacket with shoulder pads that Matthew had admired, a green shirt underneath—my color, he always said—and the jeans that I could just get into. When Matthew appeared, it was clear that he too had made an effort to look good for the occasion. He wore a clean blue workshirt, relatively clean chinos, and a stylish black Italian jacket. It was as if this were our first date and we had gone to some trouble to look properly single, elegantly casual. We wanted to impress each other. The moment I saw him I thought that maybe now, with the time that had elapsed, we would find the way to work this out.

"Ivy"—he kissed me on the lips—"I've missed you."

And I had missed him. It was all a misunderstanding. Bad timing and missed opportunity. I saw him now as I had seen him so many years ago when we first met. Youthful, his smile a bit on the crooked side, his eyes warm, friendly, inviting. I was not going to stop loving this man. Not for a long time. Maybe never. Perhaps my life would simply be tied up in loving him, whether we were together or not in some cruel, pointless destiny. It occurred to me when Matthew walked in as if nothing bad had ever happened between us, that this meeting after all these months was simply a natural outcome of everything that had gone before.

"I've missed you too," I said, "more than I knew."

"You look well. It's good to see you."

"Yes, it's good to see you." As I finished getting ready, Matthew went over to the crib, and looked down at Bobby, who was asleep. Viviana hovered nearby and I frowned at her. She gave me a fiery stare.

"I won't be late," I said as we walked out the door.

"That's good," she told me. "I've got to get home."

"She seems kind of gruff," Matthew said once we were on the street.

"Actually, she's very nice. She's just a little odd."

He shrugged. "So, how have you been? Are you doing all right?"

"Oh, I'm fine. Busy, working. And you? How's your work? How have things been?" I wondered how long we would dance around each other with these formalities.

"Oh, good in fact. I've got some interest from the Walker. And I have a new commercial account. I'm doing some work for Bloomingdale's, if you can imagine."

I could imagine. "What's the Walker interested in?"

"Oh, the Hall of Fame series, only enhanced. Maybe a show of Americana. I'd have a room to myself. If they go ahead with the exhibit."

"Well, that is exciting." Who, I wondered would accompany Matthew to the opening of his show at the Walker. I could see us, arm in arm, Bobby toddling between us.

"Yes, and you?"

"Oh, I'm painting. Most of those abstracts with the faces. I'm doing a desert series." He had always been interested in this side of my life. "New objects seem to be entering the work. A baby bottle for one," I said with a laugh. *"Spilt Milk,* I call that painting. I keep thinking I should make new slides."

"I'll do that for you. I'd be happy to help you make new slides."

"Well," I said, shying away from this burst of enthusiasm, "we'll see."

I ordered spaghetti primavera from the light menu and Matthew ordered a fettucini with sun-dried tomatoes and wild fungi, the kind of dish I might have ordered before I had a child. I could have eaten anything before I had Bobby and never gained an ounce, but now I seemed to have pounds sitting around my waist. It felt as if old age had abruptly settled in. I was exercising less.

"So," I said, "are you seeing anyone?"

Matthew rolled his eyes. "Ivy, please. What's that got to do with anything?"

"I don't know. I just assumed you'd be seeing someone by now."

My pasta had arrived, but I was merely picking at it. I'd ordered a glass of milk, remembering a woman in the maternity ward, her back in a brace, her body broken, because her child had taken all her calcium away. But the food was tasteless to me. I seemed to eat without eating. Meanwhile Matthew ate heartily, using a piece of bread to wipe up his sauce, washing it down with great gulps of wine.

"Why did you want to see me?" I asked.

"Why?" He looked at me incredulously. "Why? Because I miss you. I wanted to see if we couldn't normalize relations and see where it might take us. And because of Bobby. I want to see my son."

"And what . . . what are you willing to do?"

"To do? I don't know. Why don't we spend time together and see? It's not a rational thing, you know. But one day at a time, I'd like to try it out. Spending time with the both of you."

"What about Bobby? What if six months, a year from now, things don't work out with us again? What will your relationship be to your son? Will you still see him on a regular basis? Will you help me to provide for him?"

"You're asking me to make decisions about my feelings. I don't know. I can't say for sure. I need to think this through."

"It's the child I'm thinking about, Matthew. Not us."

He was silent. Then he shook his head. "I don't know. I honestly don't know."

"I want you to legalize your relationship to him."

"I know you want that." Matthew looked up at me. "All right. I'll do it."

"You'll take care of it yourself?"

He nodded solemnly. "I'll take care of it."

When he walked me home, he wanted to come inside, but I said no. Not yet. At the outside door I kissed him on the cheek. "We'll talk," I said. "I'm tired. I want to go to bed."

"Can't I come in?"

"Another time. Not now."

Upstairs, I found Viviana getting ready to leave. She looked at me and shook her head. "What is it?" I asked.

"It's none of my business," she said.

"Well, you're making it your business. Tell me. What are you thinking?"

"He didn't touch the baby."

"Bobby was asleep."

"I don't care," she said. "He didn't touch him." She was putting on her shirtwaist and floral skirt. "Just be careful," she told me. "See you Monday." And she was out the door.

TWENTY-SEVEN

ONCE, a few years after my mother left and we'd moved back to California, my father having taken "the cure" for his gambling and Dottie devoting herself to our care, I thought I saw my mother on Venice Boulevard. She was wearing a blue cotton dress and carrying groceries in a brown paper bag. Her skin was still pale, her black hair short, and her bearing elegant. I had hoped someday to see her disheveled, a crazy woman wandering the streets, drugged and wasted. Instead, she had a matching bag and shoes.

I was on the other side of the street and traffic was heavy, but I called to her. "It's me!" I shouted. "It's Ivy." She must have heard, because she paused and cocked her head, like a robin listening for a worm. Then she quickened her pace, tossed her groceries into a waiting car, and, before I could cross the street, was gone.

I stood perfectly still, as if the slightest movement would break the spell, and a flood of warm memories washed over me. I saw my mother holding a spoon with an egg, about to dip it into dye. I felt her take my hand as we walked through the Desert Sands trailer park. I saw the lights she strung up at holidays, despite my father's protestations that he was a Jew. I could see her face when my father told her a joke that made her laugh; the way all the harshness fell off and she was smooth and sweet as an almond.

While I stood dreaming, the woman who may have been my mother was gone from view. Maybe it wasn't she. Maybe she hadn't seen me. Or recognized me. But as I stood on Venice Boulevard, something occurred to me that I had not considered before. I'd always thought that in taking Sam and leaving me behind, my mother had made a difficult choice. Something she had struggled with over months, maybe years. But seeing her there, looking so trim and neatly dressed, made me think differently. There was not the look of anguish I'd expected to see on her face. I decided that she had left me with my father not because she thought that was fairer to all of us, but because she hadn't wanted me at all.

It was a long time since I'd given much thought to her. After she left, I used to write letters to her, but then I stopped. I'd written them as if I actually had a place to send them. I'd put her name and

Sam's on the envelope with a stamp, assuming that eventually I'd know where they should go. In the letters I answered all the unanswered questions. I completed all the half-finished thoughts. I said the things I'd been about to say when she would get up, as she always did when I spoke, and wander into another room.

I told her how we were doing. At first I told her the truth. How life was difficult without her. How I was tired of fried chicken and Salisbury steak TV dinners. How the house was a mess. About the hours I kept. About how lonely I was from dusk, when my father went on his shift, until dawn, when he returned.

But then I remembered that my mother never wanted to hear anything bad. If I told her that So-and-So's parents were getting divorced or somebody was sick, she'd say, "Oh, Ivy, you always tell me such sad things. Say something happy. Make me laugh."

So I began to make up things. "Dear Mom," I wrote, "guess what? We're moving from the trailer into a three-bedroom house, a room for each of us, a house with a real lawn. Dad's been working regular hours and putting money away. No more crazy late-night shifts. I'm doing great in school. Mostly A's and B's."

Lies, all of it lies. I spent hours alone, confronting the dilemma of what I'd do when at last she wrote to me. Which letters I would send—the truth or the lies. In the end I wasn't quite sure what was the truth and what were the lies. They all became blurred into one reality, and by the time I realized I wouldn't be hearing from her and that I'd agonized for nothing over which letters to send, I wasn't sure what had happened and what hadn't. I still wrote the letters, wondering which ones I'd send. Which would make her want to rush home more.

But after that sighting on Venice Boulevard, I took all the letters, which I'd kept in a bottom drawer, and tossed them away. It didn't matter which ones I sent. It didn't matter anymore.

TWENTY-EIGHT

MARA SAT in the middle of her bed in a flannel gown, a cup of hot cocoa in her lap. I also wore a flannel gown (hers) and had a cup of cocoa. She had put Bobby in Jason's crib, and Jason was sleeping with Alana in her little bed. I had called that afternoon to say I wanted to see her and talk and she had suggested a sleep-over. "I could use the company," she said.

We sipped our cocoa and I said, "Matthew came by again. I'm confused. He wants to see us and I suppose I want to see him. But I'm afraid."

"That he'll hurt you again?"

I shook my head. "It's not so much for me. I'm afraid for Bobby. I don't want to make a mistake for him."

She nodded. Her hair was pulled back. "I can understand that. Jason asks for his father all the time. He's very angry at me. I can't imagine what it will be like in a few years."

"I don't want Bobby to be hurt . . ." I hesitated. "Not the way I've been." Mara looked at me strangely. "There's something I need to tell you," I said. "Something I haven't told you or anyone for a long time." I smiled at her. "I hope you'll still be my friend."

Mara sucked in her lips, leaning back against the pillows. "I'll probably still be your friend." She patted my hand.

"I didn't tell you the truth when we first met. I didn't tell you the truth about my family."

"Yes," she said. "I didn't think you had."

"Why?"

She shrugged. "Too many loose threads. Things didn't make sense."

"I suppose I lied. I'm sorry about that, but it's just such a complicated story and I don't tell it to very many people." I sighed, afraid to begin. Mara looked at me, not saying a word. "I have a sister," I said at last. "Or at least I had one. My mother— my real mother, not Dottie—took her away when I was seven years old and I never saw either of them again." Mara didn't even blink, so I went on. I listened to myself speak as if I were telling a story. "My father raised me and my stepmother Dottie has been like a mother to me and most people think she is my mother, so usually I don't discuss it. I never wanted to have a child, but you see, when I got pregnant with Bobby, I couldn't do anything about it. I had to have the baby. I can't even explain why."

"You don't have to," Mara said. "I think I understand."

"I'm worried that I'm like her. Like my mother, that is. You never see me when I'm alone with Bobby. You don't know what I'm like when I'm impatient and can't take it anymore."

"We all have our moments." Now she sat up, putting the cocoa down. "I just think . . . I really think that you're a mother. Your instincts are there."

"I don't know. I can't explain it. I'm not so sure."

"You don't have to be sure. Maybe it's better if you aren't. Tell me about your mother and sister."

So I curled up beside her, and while I talked about driving home from the track with confetti in my hair and teetering at the lip of a meteorite crater, about the desert after a storm and the neon-illumined avenues of Vegas at night, Mara ran her fingers through my hair. Then I slept as soundly as I had in years.

TWENTY-NINE

THE NEXT DAY we went to the zoo. Mara's children raced around the sea lion pool while Mara and I stood watching the sea lions rise and fall. "They're beautiful, aren't they," Mara said, pointing to a leaping pup. I envied them their smooth, underwater glide. They looked so free, even though they weren't. Alana came over and asked if she could take Bobby up to the glass. "Hold him tightly," Mara said as Alana lifted him from the stroller.

The children went off to the side where the seals were climbing onto the rocks, Alana holding Bobby under the arms. "It gets easier as they get older," Mara said.

I breathed a deep sigh. "I hope so." A horde of school children arrived, shouting as a large male seal scampered high on the rocks, barking. For an instant our children were out of view. Then I heard the scream that I recognized as my son's. It was a cry I'd never before heard from him and I raced to the edge of the pool. "I don't know what happened," Alana said, speaking very quickly. "I mean, somebody bumped me and he slipped so I caught him and he just started to scream like that." Alana was sobbing as I scooped Bobby up. He shrieked again, his right arm limp as I held him.

"Oh, God, I'm so sorry," Mara said. "Alana, what happened? What did you do?"

"Mara, she didn't do anything. Maybe his arm twisted a little when he slipped. It wasn't your fault, dear." I turned to Alana, who had tears streaming down her cheeks. Jason too had begun to wail. "You guys wait here. I'll take him to first aid."

I went to a building on the side where two men sat at the barren table of the first-aid station. They were both big and burly. One was smoking a cigarette, which he put out quickly. "I don't know what's wrong with him," I said to them. They stared at me because now Bobby was utterly silent, stoical. "Something happened to his arm. He fell down and someone picked him up and he's been screaming, holding his arm behind his back."

One man told me in a thick Hispanic accent to sit with the baby on my lap, which I did, as he moved the arm gently. Bobby leaned into my chest, but not a sound came out of him. "Lady, if there were something wrong with his arm, he'd be screaming his head off now, and he's not. He's probably fine."

"You think he's fine."

"I think so," the man said. The other nodded.

I left the first-aid station with Bobby trembling in my arms. "What is it, sweetheart? Are you really all right?" Why didn't he cry when the man moved his arm? What was wrong with him?

But, though he didn't want his arm touched, he seemed better. He laughed when Alana made a fun face; he waved bye-bye to the sea lions with his good arm. We went downtown to a restaurant for lunch and Bobby slept in his stroller, but the arm still looked twisted. "Are you sure it's all right?" Mara asked, her voice concerned.

"No, I'm not sure at all."

Mara had to leave after lunch because Dave was coming to see the children, and she didn't like to be late. If she was late bringing the children, he could be late with the support payments. She touched my hand. "Do you want to go home with us?"

"No, I'm going to take a walk. I'll go to a few galleries."

"You'll be all right? Will you be able to get home okay?"

"I'll be fine," I said. They left and I sat, thinking about which galleries I would visit, when suddenly Bobby woke up, screaming. I quickly asked the waiter where the nearest hospital was, and he helped me get a taxi. I raced there.

The emergency room had a long line of people waiting to be admitted. It also had a roomful of patients waiting to be seen. There were about seventy-five people ahead of me in various states of deterioration, which appeared to result from drugs, alcohol, assorted forms of substance abuse, AIDS, homelessness, minor accidents (several had bleeding heads; it looked as if they had walked into walls). They all sat in rows of folding chairs, staring at a giant screen, watching a quiz show.

I went to look for a telephone. I called my pediatrician but he was away. The doctor covering for him, whose name sounded like Dr. Maggot, told me to go to the emergency room at New York Hospital and have an intern there report to him. I couldn't believe the wait there would be any shorter. Then I called Matthew. To my great relief he answered the phone. "Thank God you're home," I blurted. "Something's wrong with Bobby. I need your help. I can't do this alone." I told him which hospital I was calling from.

"What's wrong with him?"

"It's his arm. What does it matter what's wrong with him? I'm at an emergency room and I need help. There are dozens of people in line here."

"I could come, Ivy, but not right away. In an hour or so. Tell me, how's he doing?"

"Is it something that can't wait?"

"I'm in the middle of a shoot . . ."

"I think your son has a broken arm and there's a line around the block that I have to stand in and somebody has to help me."

"Look, I'll come as soon as I can, okay?"

Of course it made sense to me that he was in the middle of a shoot and he couldn't reschedule it. His voice sounded concerned. I couldn't expect him to drop everything. But I knew that if he were really Bobby's father, he would drop everything. He would just do it. "Don't bother," I said. "We'll be fine." And I slammed down the receiver.

I stood very still, knowing something irrevocable had occurred. Friends had told me this would happen, but I hadn't believed it. I would never again call Matthew. I would never solicit his help or try to win him over. But not for me. For the child. I had heard about mothers who lift cars off their children, who stand in the line of fire. And now it came to me, the story Patricia told me that had become a riddle, the one I couldn't solve. The one about the mother whose car stalls on the railroad track, her children inside the car. She tries to wave down the locomotive, to get it to stop, and instead the locomotive crashes into her car. What is wrong with this picture? And now I know. You fling the children from the car. Even at risk to yourself, even as the locomotive barrels down on you, you grab what children you can and hurl them clear.

I returned to the room with the wounded, the injured, the abused, the battered, the drunk and the broken, my son weeping in my arms. I joined the line for I don't know how long, waiting to reach the intake nurse, who could then give me a number so that I could sit in the room and watch the quiz show. I stood numb, the borders between danger and safety, protection and threats no longer clear, and wondered how the world survived. How did anyone survive? I patted Bobby. "It's all right," I said. "It will be all right."

At last, arms aching, I arrived. A woman with a beehive hairdo and painted-on eyebrows, sat at the desk with a sharpened pencil flicking people to the right or the left, as if she herself were judgment, as if she were the one who decided what was to happen to us all. "For you or the baby," she asked without looking at me.

"The baby," I said.

"Go to pediatrics." She waved me away with her pencil, and suddenly I was saved.

Pediatrics. Where was pediatrics? I left behind the room of the wretched and the lost and turned a corner to a wall painted with pandas and cats and elephants and giant flowers. Soft music played. The room was light. A doctor was on hand; a nurse smiled. They took me in right away. So it pays in this world to be little and helpless and small, I thought. It is only when we grow up that indifference or worse sets in.

The doctor, a smiling young resident, touched Bobby's arm, carefully moved it this way and that. "I could X-ray this, but I think I know what the problem is. Nursemaid's elbow. The bones have come out of the socket. If you hold him, I'll pop them back in."

"You will, just like that. You'll make my son well again."

He looked at me with sad, understanding eyes. "Yes," he said, "I think I can do that."

He held Bobby's arm between his hands and gave it first a pull and then a pop like a cork gun. Bobby's face opened into a startled look; he uttered a piercing scream. And then it was done. The arm moved smoothly again. The doctor and nurse stroked his head. Bobby reached with his injured arm for the animal cracker that was being offered to him. "He's fine," the doctor said, now patting my head, for I had fallen, sobbing, onto my son's hair. "He's all right. Are you all right?" the kind doctor said. "Are you all right?"

THIRTY

SOME BOYS are chasing me on their bikes. I did something to one of them, they say, and they're going to give me the dirty-girl treatment, but what I did escapes me. Maybe I took a boy's rabbit's foot or maybe I said something about one of them, but whatever it is, they're going to get me. I think, as I look back on it now, that they liked me. I'm sure of it, in fact. But whatever it was I did, they were chasing me. Maybe they thought I was pretty, with my red hair, as they chased me down the broad streets, calling my name, out onto the open road that leads to the desert.

They chase me for a long time, until my legs get weary and the sweat pours down, but I'm afraid to stop, because I don't know what they'll do if they catch me. So I keep pedaling and pedaling, and I can imagine their faces, leering behind me. I take a wide turn in order to head back toward town, and that's the last thing I remember about them chasing me. I remember only my bike going out from under me and my hands reaching out in front of me, but for what? What are they trying to grab? The air, the ground. They were beautiful, poised, as if I were diving into water and not the side of the road.

When I come to, my mother is there. She sits in the car, window rolled down, cigarette in her hand. "Get in the car," she says. "I'm taking you to the doctor. Get in. You're a mess." She rushes me to the emergency room, where a nurse with cool hands rubs my brow and a doctor removes the gravel and dirt from my legs and arms and face and my mother paces nervously around the emergency room, saying over and over again, "There won't be any scars, Doctor, will there? I don't want her to be scarred."

Later that night as we tell the story to my father and Sam, I ask my mother, "Why didn't you get out of the car? Why didn't you help me and get out of the car?"

And my mother looks at me as if I'm insane. "What are you talking about?" she says. "Of course I helped you. Of course I got out of the car. How do you think your bike got into the trunk? You didn't put it there."

That night, wrapped in bandages from head to toe, I sit up until my mother comes into the room to say good night. The window is open and a breeze blows in through the curtains, which rise and fall like ghosts. "I don't remember you getting out of the car," I tell her again.

"What are you talking about?" she asks, amazed. "I rushed right to you. I picked you up in my arms."

So why don't I remember this, even now? Why do I always see my mother sitting in that car, the window rolled down? What difference does it make if she got out or didn't? What matters is that I remember that she didn't.

I rose the next day to a snap in the weather. A heavy fog had settled in; I had always thought of the city as being immune to natural phenomena. Tidal waves could not strike our shores, earthquakes could not shatter our streets. Hurricanes would never break our glass. Of course it was ridiculous. None of us was immune.

Walking down my street with Bobby on the way to the store, I spotted a man rummaging through the garbage across the way. He was a large white man with a big beer belly, and he was collecting cans in a shopping cart. He appeared to be somebody down on his luck—somebody who had perhaps just lost a job. But what drew my attention to him more was that he had two small children with him, very close in age, perhaps four and five, and he was shouting at them as he dug into the garbage. "I told you not to do that, didn't I? Didn't I tell you to do what I said?" He handed the little girl several cans. "Don't you do that again," and as she was dropping them into the shopping cart, he struck her with his open palm across the side of her head. The little girl shrieked and he struck her again.

"I told you," he said. "You'd better do what I say. You'd better not mess around or you're really going to get it." He raised his hand again, and both the girl and her brother pleaded with him.

I had stopped, my hands on Bobby's stroller. In the fog and gray, it was not that easy to see me, but I stood perfectly still. Anger and indignation rose inside me. "If you lay a finger on that child," I shouted at him, "I will call the police. If you harm that child, I will testify in court against you."

What if he saw me across the street and came over to beat me up? What would I do then? But he did not see me. He did not know where I was or where the voice had come from. His eyes scanned the buildings and then the skies. Dropping his hand, he looked as if he had heard the voice of God.

THIRTY-ONE

MARA PHONED at nine o'clock one night. "Listen, Ivy, I have a problem." She sounded breathless. "I'm at a party in Brooklyn and my baby sitter just called. Jason is locked in the bathroom. He's hysterical. The baby sitter is hysterical. I don't know what to do. I'm getting into a cab now, but can you go over there? Call the landlord. Call a locksmith. I'll be there as soon as I can."

I heard the terror in her voice, so I wrapped up Bobby and rushed with him across the street. From the elevator, when it reached Mara's floor, I could hear Jason screaming. Oh, my God, I thought, what if he turns on the hot water? What if he scalds himself? The baby sitter, a girl about sixteen, was on her knees by the bathroom door as I came in. Alana was in a corner, sobbing. "It's okay, sweetie," the baby sitter kept saying. "Mommy will be home soon."

"What happened?" I shouted. The girl's face was white.

"He just went into the bathroom and shut the door. He locked himself in. I don't know what happened. It was an accident. It wasn't my fault."

I touched her arm. "I'm not saying it's your fault. I'm sorry. I didn't mean to shout." I handed her Bobby and grabbed a few of Jason's favorite books. "Jason, it's Ivy, Mommy's friend. Sit on the floor, Jason. I'm going to tell you a story. Here, Jason, reach for my fingers under the door. See if you can touch my hand." His fingers touched mine in the space beneath the door. I told the sitter to get the Yellow Pages while I read to Jason.

The locksmith arrived just as Mara did. Jason was sitting on the floor, his fingers still barely touching mine, as I read to him from a book of fables.

Mara came over the next morning. She carried a large box containing another batch of Jason's things. "I didn't know how to thank you," she said, "so I brought you the next installment—for next winter."

I opened the box, which was filled with sweaters, pants, pajamas. "I'm the one who should thank you," I said.

A look of sadness swept over Mara's face—the kind of look I'd seen only a few times before. "What is it?" I asked. "What's wrong?"

She sighed and was about to speak when I opened the closet where I kept Bobby's things, which was filled with clothing that had been Jason's. She went to the closet and held in her hand what had once been her son's clothes. She touched the fabrics. "Jason wore this his first Easter," she said, fondling a red suit. "And this he had on the day his father left." She ran her hands over every item. "I can remember when he wore these." She touched overalls, shirts, as if all the memories of his babyhood came spilling out of the open closet. "It's all here, isn't it," she said.

"Mara, what's wrong?" She sat at the kitchen table while I pulled on Bobby's sweatshirt. I handed her a cup of coffee and watched it turn cold in her hands.

"I have to tell you something, Ivy," she said, "but you won't like it, I'm afraid."

I sat down across from her. "Tell me, what is it?"

"I'm moving," she said at last. "I've had my apartment on the market for so long I just forgot about it. I didn't even mention it to you because I just assumed no one wanted it. But someone's made me an offer. One I can't refuse. I need the money. I can't afford the private schools. We're moving upstate to Montrose. It has good public schools, and I'll buy a little house. It's not that far." She reached across and took my hands. "You can visit on weekends."

"Weekends?" I was shaken. "I'm used to having you across the street. I don't know what I'll do."

I wanted to weep, though I couldn't explain it to her. Whose window would I look at? Whose light would I try to see in the night? Who would be there to comfort us? There would be no one to turn to in an emergency, no one to go to in need. Suddenly everything was changed.

"You'll come and visit," Mara said. "That's what you'll do."

I looked toward the window where I'd watched her, without knowing her yet knowing her, all these years. "Yes," I said, "but it won't be the same."

"We'll make it be the same."

I squeezed her hands. "We'll always be friends," I said. "Do you understand? You've clothed my child." Then I said it more emphatically. "You've clothed my child."

THIRTY-TWO

I FEEL THEM FADING; the images recede. Just as they came, so they have left, the way I always imagined ghosts would leave, or the lost souls who have at last found their rest. I have been like those people in Madagascar who dance with their ancestral bones. But now I have polished and dressed them, laid them back to rest. Like Bobby, I am learning to sleep through the night. It is as if I am a child again, learning everything from scratch. Even though I sit up with Bobby late into the night, I cannot conjure them. They've gone far away. Spirits who've left the fourth dimension. Ghosts who've moved on to rest. Or, rather, I've given them their leave.

I try to picture my mother and Sam in the various stages of their lives, but like an erotic fantasy in a person who has at last found true love, the images are played out and no longer have the power to arouse me. I do not picture them in housing tracts or bungalows by the sea. They are not on any coast in any life. When I call to them, they do not come. If they are dead or if they are alive, it does not matter much. They have become the dear departed.

I have come to the place where I must admit that what happens with most people is a mystery to me, and probably to themselves as well. And that there is no reason to try to comprehend. My mother is gone. That is a fact. She left with my sister long ago, and they won't be coming back. Try as I do to make sense of this, to find the answer so that it all comes out clear, I have to acknowledge that there are many unanswerable questions in this world, and my story will be one of them. I thought that it would all somehow become clear—a letter found in a drawer, a confession from my father, a sign, an attempt to elucidate it after all these years, but that is not the case.

I will never know why my mother left or where she went. I will only know what I can know. That there are people in this world who have cared for me and others who have not. A poet once said that our lives are shaped as much by those who refuse to love us as by those who do. I am left wondering why we give so much power to the former, so little to the latter. But I am one whose life has had such a shaping. I have had love in some of its incarnations and I have a child to take care of. These are the facts. The rest are mysteries to be solved at another time. There will be no simple answers, no sudden revelations, no miracle cures here.

At night now as Bobby sleeps, I find myself up until all hours, painting with a vengeance. And I mean exactly this: as if it will be my revenge. I draw roads I've never seen, places I've never been. I draw detailed sketches of roadside diners where I can taste the grilled cheese and French fries; I can see the waitresses with their bouffant hairdos, practically glued high on their heads. The stuffed antelope on the wall, the six-shooters crossed, framed photographs of the Marlboro man, a Navajo face.

I seem to have found this way of recording, communicating, exorcising the past. I recall my dream of the rat that wouldn't let me out of a room and realize that *rat* is *art* turned inside out. When I do not do my work, the rat takes over. On my work table now, images begin to emerge again, the contours of a woman's face. Not an abstract, really, but rather more like a picture coming slowly into focus. Around her I have painted in photographic detail as if I were some eidetic artist —memory artists, they are called—old motel keys, Chaplain on Call cards, a tornado alert, receipt from the Eureka Hotel, Eureka, Kansas. And the landscapes—dinosaur tracks, endless vistas broken only by the red flattops of buttes, a ghost town on a hill. These I draw as well.

Now I look and see the face as I had not seen it before—recognized would be a better word. It is the image I have assumed to be the fabrication of my mother's features, though from time to time other women emerged—Mara, Dottie, Sam. Now, looking more closely as I draw, I wonder how it is possible. The face has been so familiar, yet so foreign. How could I have missed it? For it is my face I see. It has been a self-portrait all along.

THIRTY-THREE

SITTING at my work table, I imagine this. Bobby is eight, and we are in a car, driving. It is like a picture I could paint with my eyes closed. We have been driving for a long time. He dozes, breathing heavily, his head bobbing from side to side. When he wakes, he stretches and stares out at the flat prairie he has never seen before. "Where are we?" he asks. The grass flows reddish and yellow. I have not seen it in years myself, but I know that beyond the grass lie the mountains and on the side of the mountains is the desert that I know. "Kansas," I tell him. "This is what Kansas looks like."

He takes out a coloring book and begins to draw. Cowboys and Indians. Horses. We bought the book for this trip. It is what he imagines the West to be. I promised him all kinds of things on this journey. Antelope, buffalo, the Navajo reservation, the Grand Canyon. So far, he has been patient with the long drive. When we stop, he eats all the hamburgers and French fries he wants. That is part of the deal.

I look at his legs and can't believe how they've grown. His hair is thick and dark. Matthew, whom he does not see, must have once had this hair. Otherwise he takes after me. People assume the man I've been seeing is Bobby's father. I met this man at an opening of my own work. When people refer to him as Bobby's father, I don't correct them. Neither does Bobby. But no one else is driving with us on this trip.

Bobby is still a child but on the brink of change. I can barely recall your babyhood, I want to tell him. Those little expressions you once said. The invisible people you believed in. The misspoken words. Once you heard my "footprints" downstairs. The wonder of discovered things. That snake you caught in your bare hands one summer in Maine. Now it is almost lost to me. We have entered this new phase. He is strong, beautiful. He still drinks chocolate milk and colors in coloring books and curls up beside me for stories at night, but each night I say to myself maybe this is it, maybe this is the last time. I'll lie down beside him, and he'll say, "Hey, Mom, cut it out." Or "I can read that book by myself." Now he plays soccer (which I've learned to like) and talks about girls with a slight look of longing in his eyes that is unmistakable. When he asks me to, I toss a base-ball with him, but even my own son says, "Mom, you throw like a girl."

We stop for the night, then drive again, then stop for another night, and soon the landscape shifts. As we drive past the lower rim of the Rocky Mountains, the land turns red, huge red buttes appear, rising out of the blood-red earth. He pauses from his drawing and looks out. "Wow, this is awesome," he says.

"Awesome," I agree.

We enter Navajo land. I know the way without looking at a map. I could drive it with my eyes closed. This land before me, red, arid, vast, is what I've always known. Let me tell you a story, I say. He puts down his book and I tell him of the ghost of Coal Mine Canyon. There are many versions of this story, but the one I've known since I was a little girl is the one my mother told me when she brought me here—about the maiden from the Bow Clan who became distraught, and nothing and no one could comfort her. One day she paused at the edge of Coal Mine Canyon, among the ghostlike rocks, and felt that her troubled spirit belonged to the beautiful canyon. Or perhaps a spirit beckoned to her.

When the Hopi discovered her body they left it where it had fallen. With the full moon her form appeared on the rocks, though this wasn't strange to the Hopi, for to them wherever someone dies, the light of the spirit shines through.

I remember the whole story. How some say that unrequited love killed her. Others, that it was the death of her son. I have walked the rims of canyons with my own mother, fearful that at any moment she might jump. In a sense I suppose she did. Now I can stand with Bobby and look down.

All time is around us, I tell him; this is what the Indians believe. He looks up at me, his face squinched the way it is when he thinks I'm putting him on. Then he shrugs, smiles, and begins to draw again. This present moment encompasses the future and the past. It's not only what the Indians believe, I tell him, touching his hand. I believe it too.

Bobby has missed some things in his childhood, but he has had others. He asks about his father from time to time, but he seems to have made peace with what we have. "I had you because I wanted you," I tell him when he asks.

THIRTY-FOUR

LATE ONE NIGHT Mara called. At first I couldn't tell whether she was laughing or crying, but then it sounded as if she was doing both. "You won't believe it, Ivy, what my day was like. I just don't know where to begin. Where to start to tell you everything that went on. It was my day to bring snack to Jason's day care center. They have this horrid system where the parents must bring the snack one day a month and you have to sign up, but what you bring is preordained. Things like blueberry granola and celery sticks. Very New Age. No sugary cake at birthday parties. Oh God, I found that out the hard way. Did I tell you? I brought a chocolate ice cream cake with apple juice, I'll admit, and the teacher, this woman named Uriel or Ariel, some ethereal spirit, she shrieks and says, double sugar, they can't have double sugar. I brought hats, blowers, cake, candles, the works, and she makes the kids gulp down the cake in five minutes and then run around the yard for an hour to wear off the chocolate.

"Anyway, that was last month, but this month, it's my snack day and it was, you guessed it, blueberry granola and celery sticks and some organic juice. I feel like I'm back in the sixties out here. Anyway, I got a late start and had to go to three stores to get everything we needed—you know, this at the health food store, that at the produce market. I was running late, and I must have hit a rock. It made a big thud under my car. I get to the school and green liquid is streaming out of the car. Just pouring out. I take Jason out of the car seat in back, grab the snack food, and race in. And there are thirty militant three-year-olds, forks in hand, already at their tables, pounding for their snacks. So I turn the food over to the teacher and head out the door, worried about the green liquid. Thinking if I take the car to the garage and it has to stay there, who'll pick up Jason at two o'clock, who'll get Alana at three o'clock?

"So I'm driving along without thinking much, except about my car, and all of a sudden these two guys in a Roto-Rooter truck come up alongside me. They're honking and waving like crazy. 'Lady,' they're shouting, 'your baby! Your baby!' So I look at where they're pointing, and there's the back door of my car open and the car seat flung up, just as if the kid has fallen out. I just wave at the guys. 'Don't worry,' I tell them. 'No problem. It's okay.' And they shake their heads, and drive away . . .

"So this is my life now," she says. "It really isn't so bad. Of course I'm lonely and maybe it was stupid to move away, but the kids are outside all day long and there's a nice duck pond nearby, and we got a puppy at the Humane Society, and really I have to say it isn't so bad."

THIRTY-FIVE

IT WAS a cold midwinter day as I made my way to Grand Central Station, weighed down as usual with Bobby's stroller, a bag for him, one for me, some gifts for Mara and the kids, and Bobby in hand, toddling along on shaky legs. "We're going bye-bye," I tell my son. "We're going away on a choo-choo for a few days." I used to think women were fools, talking to their children this way, but now I find myself mimicking them. I told Bobby we were going to see Jason and Alana and Mara and their new puppy, and though I couldn't be certain he'd remember them, he smiled at their names.

We arrived almost an hour early, so I bought our tickets and we strolled through the station, beneath its vast arching dome. We paused to buy cookies and to admire the huge photo that spanned the wall overhead, a Vermont farm complete with skaters on a pond, snowy hills, icicles dangling from a red barn, a place I promised Bobby I'd take him to someday. "Maybe we'll live somewhere like that," I said. "Would you like it? You would, wouldn't you?"

We stood in the middle of the station munching on our cookies as I explained the place to Bobby—the platforms, the clock, the tickets and trains. Suddenly there was a flurry as commuters raced for early Friday afternoon trains. People rushing in from the doors, down the stairs, pouring in from the subway. Now the station, which was empty moments before, was deluged by commuters headed for their four o'clock trains. I grabbed Bobby by one hand, stroller in the other, and braced myself against the throng.

I was happy to be going to see Mara. It was several weeks since she moved away. And I was happy to be getting out of the city. I had just begun to feel that something was behind me and something else was ahead—not just because I was making new friends or my work was getting out there again, but because I believed that somehow I had been tested and had passed, and something was over and something else was about to begin.

It was then that I saw her coming toward me. I recognized immediately the red hair, the subdued, even sad but determined—always determined—expression in those eyes. And of course the distinguishing trait—the birthmark by which I always knew I'd know her—that graced my sister's cheek. She walked quickly with her briefcase, in sneakers, Walkman on her head, racing for a train she seemed desperate to make. It was how I'd thought of her—directed toward a goal, no matter how small, often the wrong goal at that, but the one she was determined to make. Her mouth, her jaw were set, the way I'd seen them so many times when she could have told on me but never did. Yet I stood perfectly still, stunned, for in all my imaginings of her—in all my nights of sitting up, wondering about Sam—I never once thought of her here, in this city, working in these buildings, walking this pavement. Living this life.

She was coming straight at us, but of course she didn't see me. Or if she saw me, there was no way for her to know me. But I'd have known her anywhere. I would always know that face with its dark and light sides, distinct even in this crowd. I was dumbstruck and could not move. She was walking so quickly, veering off to the left, and at first I did not follow her. Before I knew what was happening, she headed in a different direction, toward a train she was about to miss.

I called, but she didn't hear. I cried out louder, but she didn't turn. Others did, dozens of people who looked askance at me. But this meeting was just as I'd told O'Malley, the detective, it would be: I'd see her face in the crowd, the face I'd know anywhere, in an airport, a shopping center, a train station, and I'd rush to her. What will O'Malley say when he hears this? I wonder. Won't he be surprised.

But she had not heard me. She had not seen me. She did not stop, but headed off like the White Rabbit, racing toward its hole. Realizing I must chase her, I started to run, but I had Bobby, and his stroller, and our bags, and didn't have the strength to lift them all off the floor.

Except for Bobby, I dropped everything, leaving it in the middle of Grand Central, as I ran after my elusive past. But I was losing her. If only I could run faster. If only I could put Bobby down, just for a few moments, I could catch her. I recalled the old ethics problem, the one I'd confronted in high school. If you are fleeing a burning building, what do you take with you? A rare painting or the cat? I'd always answered the painting. I figured you could always get another cat. But now I had Bobby and I would not put him down.

People looked at me as if I were mad when I started to run across the expanse of the station, pushing through rushing commuters, trying to get to the gate through which Sam had disappeared. I shoved people aside. I raced toward tunnels, but there were so many gates, so many trains, so many ways to go and turn. Still, I couldn't catch her. Once more I thought that if I put Bobby down, just for a moment, I could overtake her. But this was not possible. This was not something I would do.

Standing there with my son in my arms, I lost her again, if, in fact, she was ever there. Apparition, mistaken identity, or the real thing—I would never be sure. Perhaps I'll come back to this spot, empty-handed and expectant, each Friday, hoping she'll take the same train. Or perhaps I won't, for I'll have other places to be and other things to do. And maybe it's just this once that she's taking this train. If I do come back, maybe I'll find her, and through her find the way to my mother. But for now she is lost to me once again, and no matter where I go or turn, somehow I am alone, even though I hold my son in my arms.

It all comes sweeping over me and—as if it has just happened—I miss my mother. I want to run my life back like a film and rewind it so that she can see me grow up, be with me as I go off to school, leave home, marry. I want to make it all happen again so that she can watch Bobby on an evening when I go to a movie with a friend. I want to start it all over at the beginning as if my life thus far were merely a dance routine still in rehearsal, not one I was expected to perform on the stage.

I want to tell all this to my son. About the night she took me to Moon Mountain and we slept beneath the stars. I miss her, but not really the one I lost. Rather I miss the one I never had, the one I am trying to become. But he is too young to understand. I put him on the ground and he walks haltingly, holding my hand. He is light, as if he could float, rise away, above me, like a hot-air balloon. But he doesn't go. Instead, he stays, clinging to my fingers, and I clasp his. It is a gentle holding, not a desperate grasp, in this carefully poised balancing act.

Returning to where I dropped my bags, Bobby toddling beside me, I sigh, gazing upward, tears in my eyes. Then I notice the ceiling. The stars and constellations of the zodiac shimmer in the dome of the station, and I find myself standing, for the first time in so many years, beneath the night sky. Cancer, Pegasus, Orion, Taurus. Hercules, the Immortal Child. I can still name them all.

Now with my son's hand I trace the shapes of the constellations, the way the ancients did, the ones they used to navigate their course, as if in so doing I can recover the past. I draw a crab, a horse, an archer, a bull. I move his hand gently across the sky and whisper into his ear the names of the constellations, the ones I recall, and wait as he struggles to repeat them.

Mary Morris was born and raised in Chicago. Her previous books include *Vanishing Animals and Other Stories,* which was awarded the Rome Prize by the American Academy and Institute of Arts and Letters; the novel *Crossroads; The Bus of Dreams,* a collection of stories that received the Friends of American Writers Award; and the novel *The Waiting Room.* She is also the author of two works of travel nonfiction: *Nothing to Declare: Memoirs of a Woman Traveling Alone* and *Wall to Wall: From Beijing to Berlin by Rail.* She lives in Brooklyn, New York, with her husband and daughter.